Jimmy McSwain is a [private] detective, operating out of Hell's Kitchen, the rough and tumble neighborhood he grew up in. At age fourteen, he watched as his NYPD father was gunned down. Now, at age twenty-eight, gay, Jimmy has never given up pursuit of whoever killed him. But a PI must make a living, and so he's taken on the case of missing heir Harris Rothschild, whose overbearing father doesn't approve of his "alternate" lifestyle. Tracking down Harris is easier than expected, but the carnage that follows isn't. With a shocking murder on his hands, and a threat coming from some unforeseen person, Jimmy's caseload is suddenly full, and very dangerous.

Featuring a roll call of some of the best writers of gay erotica and mysteries today!

Derek Adams	Kyle Adams	Vicktor Alexander
Z. Allora	Simone Anderson	Victor J. Banis
Laura Baumbach	Ally Blue	J.P. Bowie
Barry Brennessel	Jade Buchanan	James Buchanan
TA Chase	Charlie Cochrane	Karenna Colcroft
Jamie Craig	Ethan Day	Diana DeRicci
Vivien Dean	Taylor V. Donovan	S.J. Frost
Kimberly Gardner	Kaje Harper	Stephani Hecht
Alex Ironrod	Jambrea Jo Jones	DC Juris
AC Katt	Thomas Kearnes	Kiernan Kelly
K-lee Klein	Geoffrey Knight	Christopher Koehler
Matthew Lang	J.L. Langley	Vincent Lardo
Cameron Lawton	Anna Lee	Elizabeth Lister
William Maltese	Z.A. Maxfield	Timothy McGivney
Kendall McKenna	AKM Miles	Robert Moore
Reiko Morgan	Jet Mykles	Jackie Nacht
N.J. Nielsen	Cherie Noel	Gregory L. Norris
Willa Okati	Erica Pike	Neil S. Plakcy
Rick R. Reed	A.M. Riley	AJ Rose
Rob Rosen	George Seaton	Riley Shane
Jardonn Smith	DH Starr	Richard Stevenson
Christopher Stone	Liz Strange	Marshall Thornton
Lex Valentine	Haley Walsh	Mia Watts
Lynley Wayne	Missy Welsh	Ryal Woods
Stevie Woods	Sara York	Lance Zarimba
Mark Zubro		

Check out titles, both available and forthcoming, at
www.mlrpress.com

HIDDEN
IDENTITY

The Jimmy McSwain Files

ADAM CARPENTER

mlrpress

www.mlrpress.com

Copyright 2014 by Adam Carpenter

Published by
MLR Press, LLC
3052 Gaines Waterport Rd.
Albion, NY 14411

Visit ManLoveRomance Press, LLC on the Internet:
www.mlrpress.com

Cover Art by Deana Jamroz
Editing by Jerry Wheeler

Print format: ISBN# 978-1-60820-939-2
ebook format also available

Issued 2014

Case file #101: THE FOREVER HAUNT

When tragedy invaded his life and forever changed him , it occurred during that tenuous time between boyhood and manhood, and what he remembered first and always were the sounds and smells, the strangled cry of agony, the whiff of cordite from spent ammunition. He would hear the explosion and then the exclamation, he would remember them both as though linked by that moment in time, the utter terror of his own screams that would keep him awake long after on cold nights. What next came to him were surprising images, oddly peaceful at first considering the presence of violence. The lazy climb of the morning sun, the blue sky that opened up a world fresh with possibilities, that's what his father had always told him. Finally, the lasting memory fell upon him like a weighted ghost, the body arching back in shock, toppling over a corner display of fresh cut flowers, roses and violets and daisies spilling onto the sidewalk along with the water that kept them alive, now streaming past the fire hydrant into the gutter on the corner of Tenth Avenue and 47th Street. In his mind, this incident played out like an old movie, sepia-tinged with a shiny red hue, like someone had failed in coloring it. Like he was watching through one half of the 3-D glasses he'd always liked to wear as a kid.

But he was no kid, not any longer.

Not after that day.

He had screamed out for the man who was his father, all the while holding him, trying to awaken him. In the distance came the far-too-late wailing of the police and an ambulance, both of them too late, too goddamn late. For even though his father's eyes were open as though looking up at the sun, they could see only darkness, a color beyond this world. Not that bright yellow sun, not that electric blue sky, not the bitter silver tears that fell from his only son's eyes.

A policeman tried to pry him from his father's lifeless body.

"Come on, Jim, let me help you," the cop said.

That's when the boy noticed that his clothes, a simple outfit of scuffed jeans and a T-shirt, so innocent and perfect for this early spring day, were now splattered with his father's blood. Reality began to set in. This was no dream and his father was dead. Later, his mother would attempt to throw away those clothes, as though such an act could wash away all he'd witnessed, all that had stained him. But he would retrieve them from the garbage bin at the back alley of his building, and he would lock them away, save them.

Because he would remember.

And one day, he would understand why his father had been taken from him.

And by whom.

§ § §

Two agonizing weeks passed and in that slow passage of time, the fourteen-year-old boy watched as his father—a cop who dedicated his life, literally, to the city—was honored by that blue line, buried in a season that usually sprung new life, his body, if not his soul, safe now from the dangers that lurked on deceptive, sunlit streets. But on the next day, the police came around to their apartment and confessed that, despite retrieving the murder weapon, apparently dropped at the scene of the crime by a panicked criminal—murderer—they had no leads, no suspects. It was a simple robbery gone wrong, so they said, his father innocently caught in the fray. A stray bullet from a stray gun, the assailant fitting that hollow description as well. He remembered the look, if not the face.

The boy was supposed to be holed up in his room. This wasn't his business, his mother had told him, but he had sneaked into the hallway anyway because he needed to hear that there was "nothing more we can do at this time." He wanted to know what to expect from a world suddenly turned upside down, like when he hung from the monkey bars at the park on West 47th Street, the blood rushing to his head and altering his perspective. A colorless world existed, where fathers could no longer provide for their families, where his own could no longer spot him on a Saturday morning in the park.

"I'm sorry, Mrs. McSwain…Maggie. We loved our brother Joey beyond words. He was one of the best, part of our brotherhood, and while we'll never give up, right now there are other pressing cases that demand our attention.

But know this piece of truth—criminals don't change, and he'll act again. And when he does, we'll find him. He can't stay buried forever."

A strange phrase, he thought. It was the polar opposite of what his cherished father faced for eternity, and a previously unknown sense of vengeance washed over him. The last tear he would shed for his father's death slipped down his cheek. Other cases called to them, that's what they had dared to say to the widow while sitting in her cramped living room and drinking her coffee, taking advantage of her understanding, generous nature. That's what stuck in the boy's mind, reverberating for forever.

"You boys, I know you'll handle it," his mother had said, her voice empty.

But her son knew they wouldn't. They'd already admitted as much.

Something wasn't right. Why would the cops not fight to the death to avenge their own?

They left, disappeared really, and somehow life was supposed to return to normal.

Three months later as a broiling summer raged, the case of the senseless murder of Joseph McSwain, Jr. grew ever colder, just as his father's body did lying in its solemn grave, his life remembered by his brothers just as his death was seemingly forgotten by them. Something else had also disappeared during this time, the boy he'd once been.

The man standing in his place was named Jimmy.

He was me.

Case file #101: THE FOREVER HAUNT

Case Status: UNSOLVED

PART ONE

AN ANGEL IN DISGUISE

He saw the punch coming, and in the time it took to have his nose smashed, Jimmy McSwain had three thoughts. The first thought was that this wasn't the first hit to the face he'd ever taken, and the second was that it wouldn't be the last. But he was comforted by the third, which was that it would be the last one his opponent would get in.

Jimmy McSwain always had a few tricks up his sleeve.

And he was remorseless when it came to payback. That's the code he lived his life by.

Thoughts ended. Then came the thud.

Though he braced himself for the impact, the actual moment when hard flesh met soft cartilage shook him to his core, stars lighting before his eyes. He'd moved at the last minute so it wasn't a direct hit, but he went wobbly in the knees. His recovery was fast, his fist remaining strong, closed…primed. When the expected second punch came his way, he quickly raised his left arm, his thick forearm taking the brunt of the assault. He followed up with his own thrust of coiled fist. When it connected with the guy's face, he heard an awful splat and felt the spray of blood hit his face. He watched as the guy went down without further fight.

"Told you, you don't want to mess with me," Jimmy said.

"Fucking faggot," the guy replied with anger.

"Yeah, look who's talking."

His opponent was down for the count, lying in the filthy alley, his fancy suit disheveled, and not just from the fight. The guy had been busy inside, seeking sexual favors in a downstairs room. Maybe the single punch had taken him out so quickly because he was exhausted from other physical exertions. Thin streams of blood dripped from his nose, staining his white shirt, the pale smooth skin of his exposed, flabby chest. Jimmy had noticed him from the moment he'd entered the bar, sliding his tie off like a businessman on the prowl for some after-hours activity.

Yet it was barely five-thirty in the afternoon on a late winter's day. Happy hour had now taken a decidedly bad turn for Richard S. Hickney.

Dick, was how his wife referred to him.

Jimmy was amused by the double-entendre.

"Who sent you?"

"Who do you think?"

The man hesitated, wiping blood from his nostrils. "Sissy."

Again, Jimmy was amused by the double-entendre. And he was right. He'd followed him here, he'd confronted him, he'd chased after him. The fight ensued.

"Actually, even if you're right, I can't reveal my client's name. Code of honor."

"Honor, who believes such idiocy? Fucking A, who else would have me trailed? Not like I come home with lipstick on my collar."

"Not unless you were into drag queens, and from what I've seen inside this dive, you're not. You go downstairs and then go down further on a guy wearing lots of leather. A dimly lit room, shadows covering up your imperfections. Combine that with a few shots of booze, and it sets a nice mood down there, eh?"

"You don't know shit," Richard S. Hickney said.

"Sure I do. Been coming to this place for years, but of course I stay strictly upstairs."

"You're a private investigator, and you're gay?"

Jimmy nodded, smiling a row of white teeth where one of front bottom ones grew slightly askew. "Here they just call me a private dick," he replied, "unlike yours."

Humor was not on the guy's playlist today. "So what are you going to do?"

"Not hit you again, if that's what you're asking. And I would advise you to follow my lead."

Jimmy then held out his hand, offering to help the man up. He was easily forty years old, with middle-aged flab at the waist. Normally, without all that blood on his face, he might be considered good-looking. Not his type, though. Jimmy didn't go for the closeted Jersey husband who worked in Manhattan and played after closing time with whatever boy-toy he found before returning to unsuspecting wifey and the kids. Probably voted Republican.

Richard accepted the help and was soon on his feet, dusting off the grime of the alley.

"I guess I have some explaining to do," he said, hanging his head low.

"Looks that way."

"You'll be reporting back, too, I assume."

"I would like to get paid. That's how it works."

"How much?" Richard asked, his eyes lighting up at the thought of escaping unscathed.

"Sorry, don't even try it," Jimmy said, pulling out his wallet to show off his official P.I. license. "This means I'm legit, but even if it didn't, my conscience dictates my actions. So I don't do bribes and I don't sucker punch my clients."

"Just their cuckolding husbands?"

"When provoked, yes."

"You tell Sissy this will probably end our marriage and ruin my life."

Jimmy nodded. "Or maybe you'll find it liberating. Nothing worse than being in the closet. It's the one place you can't hide from yourself."

Hickney straightened himself as much as he could while standing in the back alley of a notorious West Village gay bar, his handkerchief smeared red. He looked defeated, as though he'd gone ten rounds instead of one. He had nothing further to say, so he grabbed hold of the door they came through just a few minutes ago and disappeared in the swirling lights and music that thrummed against thick walls. He would wash up, grab his coat, slink back home. What else could he do?

Jimmy waited in the falling light of dusk for a few minutes, using the time to text Sissy Hickney. Just saying he had a bit of news—full report and photographs tomorrow. His cell phone buzzed back moments later, the yellow smiley face upside down. The Hickney's lives would change tonight, but in this city so many dramas played out, it was inevitable and perhaps necessary for Dick and for Sissy. That's how the world moved. You either played by the rules or you got caught.

Jimmy was about to step back inside the bar and grab a beer.

Slings & Arrows, as it was named, had a pretty good selection of tap beers. He figured the one hard punch had earned him two beers, and then he'd see how the night went. It was Monday, a fresh week, and clearly Richard S. Hickney had needed a quick fix after a weekend of constraining suburbia. But what about Jimmy McSwain, a creature of Manhattan, who knew its alleys and lived life by his own code, his own unfulfilled desires? What waited for him tonight?

His phone buzzed again. This time a call, not a text.

So much for those beers, so much for a night of uncertainty. He knew just what to expect from this call.

"Yeah, Ma, hi," he said.

"Dinner's in an hour, your sisters are coming. Mallory needs to talk to you."

On Monday, her dark night, Ma liked to cook and have her three children at the table.

Family meant everything to Maggie McSwain, and Jimmy was not one to turn her down.

§ § §

Tenth Avenue and 48th Street had been the address of the McSwain family for nearly thirty years, Joseph and Margaret

McSwain having moved in after the birth of their third child, finally getting out from the crowded apartment of Maggie's aging, demanding mother. Sure, it was only a block and a half away from her, but at least it was theirs, a place for the NYPD beat cop and his Broadway usher wife to raise two girls and one boy, who was the middle child.

Jimmy returned to his home neighborhood of Hell's Kitchen, having taken the Number 1 train from Sheridan Square to 50th and Broadway. Darkness had finally claimed this early March night, the air cool but not as bad as it had been during the harsh, snowy February. A light wind ruffled the shock of brown hair that he wore longer than his mother liked, but hell, he was twenty-nine and didn't he get to make those decisions now? Didn't stop her from commenting, didn't stop him from enjoying a long distance relationship with his barber.

Once Jimmy got to his front stoop, he slid his key into the first lock, entering a tight vestibule of metal mailboxes and discarded flyers. Rite-Aid was having a big sale on feminine hygiene products. He didn't need them, and he certainly hoped the mood was positive enough inside the McSwain house with his mother and two sisters that he wouldn't need to run out for them. Heineken twelve packs were going for $9.99. Maybe he'd run out anyway.

He pushed through the second door and hustled up the four flights of stairs. Having lived here for as long as he could remember, Jimmy was undaunted by the number of steps and used them as a form of exercise. It's why he was in good shape, possessing tight abs and strong legs. Those legs got him upstairs in no time and soon he was walking into the apartment, smelling steaks sizzle on the stove.

"Hey, Ma."

Maggie McSwain poked her head out from the kitchen. "You're late."

"Subway was slow."

"Hmm, your usual excuse. Where'd you stop?"

"Ma, I was on a case," he said.

"You picked up your phone, means you're not on a case. Where'd you stop?"

She knew him so well. He'd actually gone back into Slings & Arrows for one brew.

"Never mind," he said, opening up the fridge to extract a bottle of Heineken. His mother must have used that flyer already, stopping at the Rite-Aid on Eighth Avenue not far from the theatre she worked at. He popped the top and took a long pull.

"You forget something?" Maggie asked.

Of course he had. Jimmy leaned over and planted a peck on her cheek.

"You're hurt."

"I'm fine."

"You always say that."

"I'm breathing. Walking."

"In that case, you need a shave, and your hair is too long."

"Ma, I had a case. How I look doesn't matter. You, on the other hand, look great."

She waved off his attempt at sucking up. "My day off. I mostly sat. I walk those stairs enough, eight shows a week," she said, "Speaking of, you need a little pocket money? I got two shows for you, Wednesday night and Friday night."

"I'm late both shows?"

"You think my staff takes off on early shifts?"

Maggie McSwain worked as the head usher, what the old-timers called the Chief, at the Harold Calloway Theatre on West 47th Street between Broadway and Eighth. Her job was to make sure she had full front-of-the-house staffing for the show. The job had all sorts of crazy rules, at least to an outsider, but for Jimmy who had heard nothing his entire life but coded phrases like "early shift" and "late shift," "in between shows," and "double-shift," he was practically a veteran on the aisles.

"Mom, I told you, Jimmy's going to be working elsewhere."

Jimmy spun around to see his sister Mallory, who had just come from the bathroom. She had short dark hair and today wore a stylish green suit that highlighted her chocolate-brown eyes. At least she'd taken off her pumps in an effort to relax. But as much as he loved looking at his successful sister's fancy clothes, he was more intrigued by her comment. Mallory worked for a high-powered law firm on Madison Avenue and as a result had taken an apartment on the east side. She was the only one in the family to get out of the neighborhood. Having just wrapped up the Hickney case, work sounded good, especially if it was coming from her firm. It wasn't the first time, and they paid well.

"What do you got for me?"

Jimmy felt the light smack of his mother's hand against his head. "This isn't a business meeting. At least say hello to your sister first."

"Ow, Ma...hey, Mallory," he said, kissing her too on the cheek.

Mallory rubbed her cheek. "Ma's right, you need a shave. My gig is professional."

He never really gave shaving a thought. He guessed he'd missed the last few days, and the thick dark stubble had reached its scratchy stage. He waved off her comment, drank his beer, and was told to sit at the table. He did as instructed, taking his usual seat on one side, Mallory sitting in her usual spot too, opposite him. When Maggie saw the last chair empty, she rolled her eyes and called out.

"Meaghan, dinner!"

No response, and another minute went by, the chair still empty.

"I'll get her," Jimmy said.

"She's probably wearing those headphone things, can't hear a damn thing."

Jimmy went down the hallway and knocked on the second door to the right. Again, he got no response, so he turned the knob and opened it. Meaghan, all of twenty-two, was lying on her bed, talking on her phone.

"Jessie said you left the floor early," she said to whoever was on the other end. She paused, smacking her gum. "I'm not telling Ma, she hates this petty crap. Hey, not my fault Jessie was late getting back. You don't leave the floor…wait…oh, hey, Jimmy."

"Dinner's ready. Ma's calling you."

"Gotta go," Meaghan said, flipping her phone off.

Soon the McSwain family was seated around the table, the four of them in the same places they'd sat in all their lives—the girls on one side, the lone boy on the other. Maggie sat at one head of the table, but the other was empty, just as it had been for more than half of Jimmy's life. They no longer kept a place setting, but Joseph McSwain Junior's beer mug still sat there as clean as if he'd just taken it out of the dishwasher himself.

Holding hands, they said grace. Then they dug into a hearty meal of steak and potatoes.

"So, Mallory, what do you have for me?"

Maggie didn't look pleased that they were discussing business, but she sat and chewed and stared ahead at the empty chair opposite her. Like she was commiserating with the man who should have been there.

"Missing person, actually."

"Oh, cool," Meaghan said. "Runaway wife? Angry child? Paternity issue?"

Meaghean watched too much Jerry Springer and Maury Povich in the afternoons. She had a lot of free time during the days since she worked her nights and weekends alongside her mother at the theatre.

"Ignore her," Jimmy said.

"Story of my life."

"Meaghan, let your sister talk."

Peace restored, Jimmy continued. "What else can you tell

me?"

"Actually, one of the senior partners wants to discuss it with you," she said.

"Why me?" Jimmy asked, skeptical now that it involved someone rich. Rich people liked to hire the poor to help them navigate dirtier worlds.

"Because I recommended you," she said.

"Let me guess," Jimmy said, "whoever is missing, he also happens to be gay."

Mallory sipped her wine, but she nodded.

"Look at that, Jimmy, you've got good gaydar," Maggie said. She had no problem with Jimmy's sexual orientation and she was always trying to fit in.

"No, Ma, that's not what that phrase means." Meaghan said. "Gaydar is, like, when you try and guess if someone's gay or not. Like Chad at the theatre…"

"Oh, he's just a nice boy," she said.

The three McSwain siblings laughed, and Maggie waved off their nonsense.

"So, Jim, anything you can do about that bruise on your nose before morning?"

"Guess I can cover it with L'Oreal," he deadpanned.

They talked more as they ate, a congenial family who clearly enjoyed sharing meals and time together. Maggie would have it no other way. "Who's going to want dessert?" she said, her chair scraping against the floor.

Jimmy was already thinking about a bigger dessert, a huge payday from a hot-for-shit law firm. "So, where should I meet you, and when?"

"Tomorrow, noon. You'll have lunch with Mr. Rothschild and his wife. They want to discuss their son with you."

"I repeat, why me? And I mean the real reason."

Mallory waved off his suspicion. "Let's just say you two have something in common."

Jimmy nodded. He was guessing the Rothschild's son was gay. As though like knows like, and a straight P.I. wouldn't be able to help.

Mallory continued. "Eighty-second and Fifth. Wear a tie."

"Anything else?" Jimmy asked.

Maggie whistled as she set down an angel-food cake in front of them. "Jimmy, you dress nice and professional and don't forget to shave. You want the job, dress like it."

Sometimes she made Jimmy feel like he was ten years old. But if that was the case, he would be able to glance at the end of the table and see his ruddy-faced father downing a Pabst Blue Ribbon beer while saying, "Saints alone, leave the poor boy to himself, Maggie, you're gonna turn Jimmy into some nancy-boy if you keep that up." But Joey was gone, so he listened to his mother, and how about that? He was a nancy-boy anyway.

"Yes, Ma."

"Jim, why not wear one of those nice suits Remy gave you," Meaghan said.

Silence fell over the table until Jimmy slammed his fork down. His brown eyes darkened further as he stared daggers at his annoying sister. Leave it to mother McSwain to come to the rescue. She knew just how to steer the conversation away from unpleasant topics.

"This job Mallory's got for you, Jimmy, I think it's what they would call paydar."

CHAPTER TWO

"So, Jim, another?"

Jimmy looked down at his near-empty pint glass, the remnants of his Smithwicks staring back at him. He'd had the one beer in the Village and another when he got to his mom's, but it long since been absorbed by his mother's heavy food, so he'd had another Heineken after dinner. Maybe he'd had enough for a Monday night, but then again, he was sitting at the edge of the bar now, past eleven o'clock, diligently working up the report for Sissy Hickney about her husband's wandering dick. It was depressing to think about the heartbreak and anger across the river in the Hickney household, how it would affect their kids when they found out their parents were likely divorcing. Parents should suck it up and stay together, Jimmy believed. No point in denying the kids what they deserved.

"Sure, hit me," he said, thinking about his nose and regretting his choice of words, "and a shot of Jameson's. Thanks, Paddy."

Patrick "Paddy" Byrne was the rotund, seventy-ish bartender and owner with the crooked smile and broken capillaries on his nose. He'd been at it a while and he simply nodded, used to the extra requests of men who wished to bury whatever demon lived inside them.

Paddy's Irish Pub was on the west side of 9th Avenue and 43rd Street, a dark hole in the wall place where the regulars gauged your mood by what you ordered. Jimmy ordering a shot said it all. That's why the Monday night gang was leaving Jimmy alone as he tapped away at his laptop, lost in a world of detection, betrayal, and lies. The shot arrived, he knocked it back hard, then set the glass down on the scuffed old bar with a clack.

He'd been trailing Richard Hickney for two weeks, and while he had provided the wife with updates, this was to be his final report, a comprehensive study of her husband's after-work activities. Some of which were innocent, like sharing a couple of drinks with some co-workers, while other nights, he'd witnessed the guy trolling for sex in places of questionable repute. One night it was a trendy gay bar in Chelsea, the next a crimson-soaked Lower East Side underground club that had been raided by cops more than once, and now tonight, an old-style pick-up joint in the West Village. Each time Dick Hickney had met up with someone and indulged his hidden attraction to men. What he was up to hadn't been much of a surprise. His wife had said she always suspected, but she'd gone through with the wedding ten years ago anyway and had a kid with him. Once she read this report, her inner fears would be confirmed. Her husband was gay, bi at best, and her life was a mess.

Now with a fresh pint of Irish ale set before him, Jimmy looked up from the bright light of the screen before taking a sip, and felt his worries over the Hickneys dissipate as the cold brew slid down his throat. Enough of their troubles. They were not unlike so many households in this city and across the Hudson, heck, across the country. Motives were kept locked inside people's minds, lives were forever changed behind closed doors. Speaking of closed, he shut his laptop, turning it and, hopefully, his mind off for the night.

He zeroed in on the Monday night action at Paddy's.

A decent crowd had gathered. Weathered-looking guys who worked the docks gathered their thick coats about them, murmuring obscenity-laced dialogue that went nowhere, all while staring up at the large flat-screen television—Paddy's one concession concession to modern times. Two jovial, well-suited guys on ESPN were recounting the day's baseball action. Spring training was in full swing. Jimmy thought the guy on the left side of the anchor desk was kind of hot in a nerdy, academic way. Jimmy was rough around the edges, so sometimes he liked a bit of refinement. Then he looked away, instead concentrating on a game of darts being played in the back, the high-fives and booze-fueled dares coming from a mixed crowd of loud-mouthed women with dyed-blonde hair and unkempt guys with beer bellies trying to lure them into their meaty, desperate grasps. The daily dance of seduction, Jimmy surmised, blue-collar, hard-working, straight folks getting more attractive with each beer they drank.

It wasn't his usual scene, but Paddy's was family.

But then again, these days he wasn't sure what his scene was. He thought back to Slings & Arrows and the come-hither looks unfolding between men there, too. Not that dissimilar to Paddy's, lost souls of humanity looking for a bit of companionship, gay, straight, somewhere in between, it didn't matter. Some people just felt the need to be touched, comforted. Who would comfort Sissy Hickney after she read his report, after she had stared for too long at the photographs Jimmy had snapped as her husband kissed another man? Conclusive proof of her husband's homosexual infidelities.

"Jim, you seem down," Paddy said.

"Guess I'm just not in the mood…for this," he said, waving his hand in the air.

He nodded. "Anniversary's is coming up, isn't it?"

Jimmy took a large gulp of his Smithwicks. It tasted bitter. "Ten days," he said. "Not that I'm counting."

"You need something—and I don't mean a refill—you know who to talk to."

Paddy Byrne wasn't just the proprietor of his own bar, he was Maggie's brother, making him Jimmy's uncle. He'd been the sole male figure in Jimmy's life since that day years ago when his father had been killed not in the line of duty. And while Paddy's wizened presence was comforting, it wasn't the same as having the boisterous Joey around. But since then, Paddy had listened. He'd watched as Jimmy had grown up, he'd seen the boy-into-man struggle with his inner demons, with his sexuality. Paddy offered no judgments. He was old school, but that didn't mean he was close-minded.

"Thanks, Paddy."

"How's your mother?"

"She made dinner tonight."

"Her three kids at her side, so for now she's content."

"I'll bring her by soon."

He nodded. "You staying at your Ma's tonight?"

"Thought I'd just retire to my office. Got to file this report. New case tomorrow."

"Business is good," he said, wiping his hands on a dirty dishtowel.

"Some might say that's a bad reflection on society," Jimmy said.

"Oh, you are in one, aren't you?"

Paddy patted his rough cheek before moving on to pull the beer taps for happier patrons. Jimmy downed the last of his pint, gathered his laptop under his arm and waved goodnight. The laughter he heard as he closed the door behind him wasn't directed at him, it was just life taunting him. Let down your guard, just have a bit of fun, don't carry the world in your back pocket, that's what he interpreted.

Jimmy unlocked the door next to the bar, let himself in, and climbed the two floors to the front apartment, the official-for-tax-purposes office of Jimmy McSwain Investigations. No black stenciling on the door, no beveled glass. Just a door and, inside, a desk, a sofa that pulled out into a bed, and a small fridge stocked with beverages. He set the computer down on his desk, and looked around at the empty walls and barren furniture. A clock on the wall ticked, edging ever closer to midnight.

Good. Send this day packing, he'd seen enough.

He pulled the cushions off the sofa and pulled out the bed. The flimsy mattress stared at him, as uninviting as always. But this place was his only respite from the world, a quiet retreat from his mother's endless questions about his job and from his sister Meaghan's constant gum chewing and endless chatter on her cell phone. Jimmy McSwain liked to keep his life as free of complications as he could. Keeping a clear head and his mind on business, that's what drove him.

But that didn't mean he wasn't human, that he didn't crave companionship and security, and deep inside him he wondered if he'd ever find the kind of happiness shared by the lucky ones. He thought of his sister's remark about Remy and, for a moment, the man's face flashed before him, and a feeling of sharp regret hit him hard in the stomach. Which then made him think of the hit he'd taken to his face earlier. His jumbled mind pictured Richard and Sissy Hickney signing divorce papers.

Jimmy felt the walls close in on him, which in this tight studio meant something. He left the apartment and went back into the cold air of early March.

His feet knew where he was headed before the rest of him did.

§ § §

Gaslight couldn't have been more opposite Paddy's, both in style and in clientele.

The bar was sleek and modern, lots of metal that gave off a chilly reception.

Located just around the corner from Paddy's, the wide open space was also filled with men and only men, except for the occasional fag hag who for some reason loved hanging out at a bar with no chance of going home with anyone. Jimmy pushed his way through the door, smiling at the bouncer as he did so, and he was immediately affronted by the dreamy melody of "I Dreamed a Dream" from *Les Miserables*. How could he have forgotten, tonight was Musical Monday at Gaslight, which meant the DJ spun tunes from any assortment of Broadway shows, and the guys sang along like they were at some Equity audition. Theatre was the other side of Jimmy's life, far from the sometimes unforgiving world of private investigation. He'd been a part of it as long as he could remember, some nights hanging out at the Calloway Theatre until the last patron had left the house, walking home hand in hand with his tired mother, happy memories of whatever show was playing swirling in his impressionable mind. He'd heard the tunes of Coleman, Porter,

Sondheim, Lloyd Webber; he'd absorbed the poetry of Williams, O'Neill, Odets, Pinter.

As the overplayed ballad reached its emotional crescendo, Jimmy sidled up to the horseshoe-shaped bar, ordered a Bass Ale from a hunky blond guy who was mouthing the lyrics. Jimmy took his first sip as the Gwen Verdon version of "Hey, Big Spender" from *Sweet Charity* began, and, feeling like the song was aimed at him, he left a two-dollar tip. Then he moved on and found a spare corner of the bar where he could cool his heels by himself, survey the scene, and enjoy the campy music. He actually didn't mind listening to show tunes. He supposed it was the one gay stereotype he embraced, but don't ask him to go to a Streisand concert. She rubbed him the wrong way.

He recognized several regulars, not that he would classify himself as one, but he'd been here often enough. Monday night Broadway was mostly dark, so it gave the chorus boys a night off from the rigors of performing. So what do they do? Hang with friends, drink, sing songs, flirt, and, in some cases, go home with someone. Jimmy watched it all play out like a well-choreographed scene, sipping at his beer, knowing he didn't need one but what was he supposed to do? Drink water? Sliding a hand into his pocket, attempting a look of indifference, he tapped his shoe to something from *Rent*, and that's when he saw a guy coming his way.

"Hi," he said.

"Hey," Jimmy said, taking a sip at his beer as he assessed who had approached him. Even with just the one word expressed, he thought he detected an accent coming from the noticeably cute guy. He was probably five-nine, slim of frame with a thin blond beard and wire-framed glasses. He was bookish-looking and Jimmy expected patches on the elbows of his blazer. He carried a martini glass that was half-drained of some pink liquid.

"You like show tunes?" the guy asked.

"I'd have walked out the moment I arrived if I didn't," Jimmy said.

"Long way to say yes."

Jimmy smiled. Definitely an accent, English. He extended his hand. "Jimmy."

"Barry," he said.

"Like Manilow? Or Gibb?"

"Neither of them is English."

"Humphries?"

"Are you saying I look like Dame Edna?"

The two of them laughed, their musical and Broadway pop culture references drawing them closer.

"Besides, Barry Humphries is also Australian."

"Sorry, don't know any English Barrys."

"Now you do," he said, rather cheekily. "So, Jimmy, got a husband?"

So, it was the direct approach. "No," he answered.

"Wife?"

He thought of Sissy Hickney. "Uh, no."

"Boyfriend?"

He preferred not to go down that dark path, because that's where Jimmy's life got thorny. "Definitely not," he replied flatly.

"I sense something there."

"Move on, next question?"

The guy drank his martini, smiling when he was done. "Got a fuck buddy?"

Now that was being forward. Jimmy decided he liked the approach and leaned in closer to Barry. His eyes flashed. "Something tells me I could if I wanted."

"Hell, you could have whoever you wanted. You're...hot," Barry said. "You're different from the other guys here, not that they're not, but..."

"They know the lyrics a bit too well?"

"I saw you when you walked in, you had this…swagger about you. Not quite trouble, but a sharper edge the gym bunnies here lack. Now that I see you up close, you look like your nose had an argument with someone's fist."

Jimmy nodded. "You should see the other guy."

"No thanks, I like this view just fine."

This was definitely going somewhere. Eventually, probably to Jimmy's bed.

They took up at a vacant table, their backs against the wall. Some young guy was belting out "Corner of the Sky" from *Pippin*. They talked. Barry was visiting from England, here on a three-month job exchange at Penguin Books, and he'd only just arrived last weekend, surviving his first day. But that was as settled as he'd gotten. He was still living out of a suitcase at a friend's apartment while he waited for his sublet. The message was clear: no going to his place. Either the beer was getting to Jimmy or the drains of the day had won out, because after they had shared another drink and taken the simmering heat of their flirting to a higher heat, he suggested that if Barry wanted to come home with him, he could.

Barry leaned in and kissed him, a hand snaking inside the open collar of Jimmy's shirt. Jimmy felt a stir in his loins as Barry stroked the exposed triangle of chest hair.

"You're sexy, Jimmy."

"Is that a yes?"

"Yeah, that sounds great," he said.

The kiss had felt nice to Jimmy, surprisingly sweet for a pick-up.

They left together moments later to some envious glances from the show tune singers, and as Barbra Streisand began "Don't Rain on My Parade," Jimmy realized he'd escaped just in time, and in the company of a nice, funny guy with a charming accent. They made their way down Manhattan's darkened streets, mostly in silence, back toward Paddy's. Soon they were walking up the stairs to Jimmy's office. He opened the door and allowed Barry first entry into the apartment. Jimmy switched on a lamp for a bit of mood lighting and Barry laughed, pointing toward the open sofa bed.

"Expecting company?"

"I almost turned in a while ago."

"I'm glad you didn't."

Jimmy preferred to say nothing, turning unspoken words into action.

They fell on the bed fully-clothed, the thin mattress hardly a deterrent to their desires. They were focused on each other, sweet kisses turning hungrier, the stubble of his chin scraping Barry's beard, eager hands fumbling with buttons and zippers, and soon those kisses intensified further as their heated, naked bodies became entwined in a mess of limbs. Jimmy soon had positioned him on his back, lifted his legs, and with the guy's eyes pleading, entered him with an eager thrust.

"Oh yeah...Jimmy, just...wow, perfect," Barry said, exhaling at the impact.

Their syncopation grew even more perfect, the two men's motions in rhythm, like they'd found their own corner of the sky, and they moved and they thrust and they embraced and they cried out in the quiet of the small office. Jimmy's mind cleared itself of his troubles as his hips took over, concentrating on the demands of the cute guy, his urgings as well as his own building desire. He felt Barry's fingers slide along the mat of hair, pulling at it gently, making his cock harder, thicker. When the rush of orgasm hit him, Jimmy's hard body contorted in a delightful paroxysm. Barry was not far behind, and soon the two of them were done. Jimmy shot his load into the condom, while a white rope of jizz splattered Barry's hairless chest. Both of them stared at the ceiling as their heated passion cooled.

Barry slid in next to Jimmy, cuddling him, again displaying surprising tenderness. Barry absently brushed at the generous mat of dark hair on Jimmy's chest. He admitted to having taken note of his chest at the bar, proving his point by seeking out an erect nipple hidden beneath the dense hair. He licked it, flicked it with his tongue. Jimmy felt his cock harden again.

"What is this place, anyway, your apartment?"

"Office, really," Jimmy said.

"Yeah, you didn't really tell me what you did. You were kind of evasive."

"I'm a private investigator," Jimmy said, more to the darkness than the light beside him.

"No shit, really?"

"No shit," Jimmy said.

"Were you working a case tonight?"

"I was off duty," Jimmy said.

"Were you a cop? Did you go all rogue and quit?"

The way Barry spoke made Jimmy sound like a stock character in a movie.

The real reason went far deeper. But that was for another time.

"Graduated from the academy, but nope, never wore the uniform," Jimmy said, a catch in his throat. Swallow it, move on. They'd shared their bodies, but he wasn't opening his heart, not now, not yet. "I trained as a P.I. under a former detective. Got my license, struck out on my own as soon as the law allowed."

"Why'd you want to be a P.I.?"

"Kind of private, why," Jimmy said.

"That a play on words?"

Jimmy attempted a smile, but it faltered. "Not intentional."

"Sorry, didn't mean to pry."

"Some things I don't share on the first encounter."

"Right, got that."

Jimmy knew he'd shifted the night's playful tone and wished

he could take it back.

Barry said, "So, probably I should leave."

"You don't have to."

"You're a complicated guy, Jimmy."

He blinked and turned to Barry. "Sorry if I scared you...or whatever, about my job."

"I think it's exciting. Some guy really punched you today, didn't he?"

"It's okay, I got the last one in. Last several, actually."

"Tough guy," Barry said with a sexy grin.

"That's me."

"And yet I find you at a bar where they're playing show tunes."

"At the end of the day, you're another day older."

"Wiser?" Barry asked.

"Hardly ever."

Silence again fell between them, this time more comfortable. Finally, Barry said, "A gay private eye. I guess you've heard all the dick jokes, huh?"

"You could say that," Jimmy said.

"What else do you want to say?"

"Nothing," Jimmy replied.

"Good. I want you to fuck me again."

Barry opened himself up, this time climbing atop Jimmy. He slid down on Jimmy's hard cock, then began to rock up and down, his energy increasing with each motion. He rubbed his cock along the trail of hair on Jimmy's flat stomach, even as he closed his eyes. Jimmy remained focused, his eyes wide open, watching the exchange between them. They didn't speak again for quite a while, not unless the groans of pleasure that enveloped the room counted. The light now turned off, darkness swirled around them, allowing the two to exist in their own world, one where momentary passion sent the pulse of their hearts deep into the shadows. This was pure physicality, satisfied only by the release of something within them, something that couldn't help but rattle their souls.

Afterwards, fierce orgasms having rocked their worlds, it was only Jimmy staring at the ceiling as Barry slept against his chest, hair curled in his fist.

They stayed that way all night.

CHAPTER THREE

The Upper East Side always felt like another world for a street-wise kid who grew up in a place called Hell's Kitchen, as though by traveling uptown the canyons of New York opened up and showed off more of the sky's lustrous heavens. As Jimmy disembarked the subway at 77th Street and Lexington, he felt like the sun was shining more brightly, growing in intensity the further he went toward Fifth Avenue. Large, pre-war apartment buildings lined the exclusive strip, as did the eastern edge of Central Park; just the notion of money gleamed like polished gold, the glint off BMW windshields like sparkling diamonds.

Sometimes Jimmy was surprised the only difference was a zip code.

At Fifth and 84th, he walked under an awning that stretched from the building to the curb, a doorman opening the wrought-iron door as he approached. He didn't look askance at Jimmy, since he was wearing one of several designer suits that hung, mostly unused, in his closet. He'd gone for a dark blue Hugo Boss with a blue shirt and a maroon tie, which had his mother pronouncing him handsome, even with the fading bruise across the bridge of his nose. That was the only remnant that remained of yesterday. The Hickney report was emailed, and his bed emptied of the cute Englishman Barry. They'd exchanged numbers and words that suggested they'd meet up again. But his personal life could wait, business was at hand.

He found his destination, a place called The Corinthian.

Jimmy saw no Greek columns. It was just a fancy sounding name.

"I'm here to see a Mr. Rothschild," Jimmy said as the front doors were opened for him. "I believe he's expecting me."

"Your name, sir?"

This was the part of the job Jimmy hated, coming up to these gilded addresses and sounding so street when he stated his name. His parents hadn't named him James. His birth certificate was proof they never intended to call him anything but Jimmy or Jim. So, his legal name was Jimmy Joseph McSwain, and if you added in his confirmation name, he was Jimmy Joseph Byrne McSwain. Byrne was his mother's maiden name, and his choosing it had not only pleased Maggie, it had brought a wistful smile to his maternal grandmother, Nora, as well. When it came to introducing himself in such rarefied worlds such as the Corinthian, the informal Jimmy sounded inadequate.

"Mr. McSwain."

A quick phone call confirmed his appointment, and soon he was hurtling up to the twenty-fourth floor, the penthouse suite, where the elevator opened directly into the duplex apartment. A man stood at ramrod attention, his white hair and matching goatee neatly trimmed. He could have been the butler, but he also could have been Rothschild. He decided to wait until the man introduced himself.

"Ah, Mr. McSwain, Saul Rothschild," he said, extending a hand.

The two men shook, Rothschild's grip strong as he led Jimmy into the apartment.

He didn't know much about designers or fabrics, but this place looked like one of those over-decorated hotel suites found in five-star resorts. Classic elegance, smelling of money. Jimmy reminded himself to thank Mallory for not just the opportunity but for suggesting he dress well for the luncheon. How would a man like Rothschild take Jimmy seriously if he'd shown up in his usual uniform of jeans and whatever casual shirt hasn't hit the laundry pile yet? He'd even shaved, so he was fresh looking for once. He almost beamed with pride.

"Not exactly what I expected," Rothschild said.

"I'm sorry, sir?"

"You're a private investigator, right?"

"Yes, sir?"

"With that tie nearly strangling you, you look more like you just stepped out of a fashion magazine," he said. "Although the photographer forgot to airbrush the bridge of your nose. Am I to assume the other guy looks worse?"

Why did everyone go for the obvious joke? What was he supposed to say, no?

Fortunately he was spared from answering, as the two men were interrupted by the arrival of two women, one of them his sister Mallory, looking as stylish as ever. She'd come a long way from the braces and gawky limbs she'd endured as a teenager. Jimmy knew she worked hard at her neighborhood makeover, and sometimes she looked like she'd never even heard of Hell's Kitchen, much less having grown up there. She lessened the tough girl accent, coming out only when forced. In certain social circles, she probably referred to her neighborhood as Clinton.

"Jimmy, thanks for coming," Mallory said, embracing him.

"Wouldn't miss it, a case is a case," he said.

The other woman grimaced, as though the mere presence of a private investigator inside her elegant home was somehow soiling it. Should he have wiped his feet before walking onto their plush white carpet? No doubt the lady of the house, she wore a thick helmet of blonde hair and her age fell somewhere between Mallory's thirty-one years and Saul Rothschild's seasoned age. Surgery might have tipped the scales Mallory's way.

"Mr. McSwain, my wife…Jellison," Rothschild said.

"Jellison? That's…unique," he said.

She smiled, her mouth barely moving, as though she'd heard that a thousand times.

"Mr. McSwain, thank you for coming. Shall we sit down to dine? I'm famished."

She was also razor thin and Jimmy figured she might fill up just by breathing in the smell of food. But he wasn't here to judge, he was here for a job, and now that he was in the company of this seemingly typical upscale couple, he was curious why they needed his particular brand of services. As they were led into a dining room where four place settings awaited them, Jimmy exchanged a look at Mallory, but couldn't read her face. She was the conduit, the connection between the mean streets and the gilded skyscrapers. It was only her responsibility to get him here, not to fill him in on what was at stake.

Their hostess directed them to seats, and in no time a server appeared carrying a china soup tureen. The servant ladled four bowls before departing, leaving them to begin. Jimmy looked again at his sister, who was gently sipping at her soup, careful not to make a noise. He'd have to watch his manners here, not use his tie as a napkin.

"I trust you found the place all right?" Jellison asked.

"Six train to Seventy-seventh, then a short walk."

"Oh, you took the…the subway…" she said, the word iffy on her tongue. "Saul, I told you we should have sent a car."

"Nonsense, he's a capable boy."

Use of the word "boy" wasn't lost on Jimmy. Was it meant to somehow demean him, put him in his place? Or maybe for a guy of Rothschild's age, anyone below fifty qualified. Jimmy opted to concentrate on the capable part of his comment, taking it as a compliment.

"Jim's more than capable, he's resourceful," Mallory said.

"Ah, Jim, is that why you go by?"

Jimmy shrugged. "Jim, Jimmy, take your pick. When my mother's been angry at me, I've answered to worse."

"Jimmy it is," Rothschild said. "Informal is always better."

Jimmy thought it an odd statement considering their surroundings and the fact he was wearing a tie.

"Still, I insisted he dress for lunch," Mallory said.

"That's fine," Rothschild said, "but let's move back to that resourceful part."

Time for business, Jimmy thought, watching as the soup

bowls were removed and replaced by a cold lobster salad stuffed into a curved leaf of romaine, accompanied by a nice chilled bottle of some kind of white. He was told the name, but it didn't sound like any he'd heard of. Phoey-Fussy something. Taste was what mattered and it hit the spot, the bite of the alcohol allowing him to relax a bit.

"Jimmy, resourcefulness is what's needed here," Rothschild said, "but far and above, it's not the most important thing."

Jimmy waited for what that thing was, kind of dreading it. When cases got complicated, he raised his prices. He had a feeling his paydar—as Maggie had dubbed it—for this case was not quite going to buy him the apartment next door but might pay the rent of his office for the rest of the year.

"Discretion is foremost on our minds, mine and Jellison's."

"I can do discreet," Jimmy said.

"Cost is not an issue," Jellison added.

Jimmy had a feeling cost was never an issue when it came to the lady of the duplex.

"So what is the issue?" Jimmy said. No more being a wallflower, it was time to dance.

"We want you to find our son," Rothschild said.

So this was the missing person Mallory had forewarned him about. He stole a look at Rothschild, then at Jellison and tried to figure out just how old their son could be. We weren't talking a kid. Finding a grown-up man, an adult, would not be easy, especially if he did not want to be found and had the financial resources to stay hidden.

"You could hire anyone, why me?"

Jellison darted wide eyes her husband's way. He nodded, giving her permission to speak. As though she would say what he wished not to say.

"Our son is gay, Mr. McSwain," Jellison said.

Jimmy tossed Mallory a look. She shrugged helplessly.

He'd been waiting for that response. Why else had he been summoned? Only a gay P.I. could find a missing gay son, right? As the heartsick mother of the gay son spoke, Jimmy's dark, curious eyes caught the father's placid face. He made a mental note. One was supportive of the lifestyle, the other opposed, and wasn't it always the same? For a moment Jimmy thought of his own father and wondered just what kind of response he'd have gotten from the Old World Irish cop.

Probably not good.

But no sense going there, not really. Fantasy filled minds, reality hit hearts.

Like Rothschild had intimated, this wasn't about judgments, not about him, not about her, and surely not about Rothschild Jr. This was a job, a case, pure and simple, and Jimmy was damn good at what he did. So, he set down his wine glass and wiped his mouth of any trace of food, reminding himself of his manners. Immersed as he was in this fancy world he knew so little about, he knew they wanted him more for the life experiences he was familiar with.

"Tell me more."

§ § §

Lunch took priority, so Jimmy ate and drank along with his sister and his hosts and listened to polite talk of the weather, political turmoil, and the mess the Upper East Side had become during the endless building of the long-rumored Second Avenue subway. Jimmy was not convinced the Rothschilds had been east of Park recently, unless in a car that was taking them to JFK. But he nodded politely, inserted comments when appropriate, and finished his lime sorbet with a scrape of his spoon.

"So, shall we retire to the living room and get down to business?"

Mr. Rothschild might have spoken the words, but once Jimmy was sunk into the soft floral pattern of the sofa, it was Jellison Rothschild who took over. Her husband was nowhere to be seen, nor was Mallory.

"Mrs. Rothschild, like I said before, tell me more."

"His name is Harris," she said.

"Harris Rothschild?"

"Yes, whatever else would it be?"

Jimmy had taken out a notepad. "Facts are important, Mrs. Rothschild. Not all family members share last names."

"Call me Jellison," she asked.

Jimmy wasn't sure his tongue worked that way. He'd keep things neutral. "I don't wish to be impertinent, but Mr. Rothschild does look a bit older than you, I was just wondering if your son was from a previous marriage or…"

"…Or?"

Jimmy flushed red, wishing he hadn't gone down this path. But she wouldn't be the first of his clients to lie to him, and he had to dig into every crevice no matter what bit back when he pushed too far. Jellison leaned forward, her opaque nails touching his hand. He didn't pull back, just let her rest them there.

"Mallory tells me you're gay," she said.

"Is that an important detail?"

"For finding my son, I think so."

"How so?"

"If you have to go into places of…well, places where gay men congregate, isn't it easier to hire someone who's comfortable going into them?"

"I'm not sure what places you mean."

"Bars…clubs…those kind of places you find, you know, downtown."

He wondered if Jellison's ivory tower ever changed colors.

"Fine, let's move on."

But she wouldn't, her eyes now focusing more on Jimmy. "You're quite handsome," she said, "and, if I may, you look a bit…not quite dangerous, but you have this edge to your aura, perhaps anger inside you. You are not at all like Harris."

"Mrs. Rothschild…uh, Jellison, let's concentrate on Harris. I'm just the hired hand."

She seemed to respond to such a classification, as though he were speaking her language.

"I may make it sound like Harris is a boy, unsure of himself, lost somewhere in a world he doesn't understand or belong in," she said, "but in truth, he's as capable and resourceful as you. He's headstrong, always has been, not unlike his father, but he's sensitive—overly so. Like there's two of him. He knew he was gay…my God, I think he was trying on my shoes when he was five. Not just trying them on, walking in them, and better than me. Pumps were his favorite, the higher the heel the better. Saul hated watching him parade around the apartment, but what could he do? Anytime I came home with new shoes, Harris was all over them and the way his smile would light the room, it was like he had finally found comfort in his own skin. Give him a baseball… he was lost."

"I get it," Jimmy said.

Jimmy had trophies in his room back home from his summer days playing baseball as a teenager. He'd been a stud pitcher, and he threw like the angry young man Jellison had correctly assumed he was. High heat that made the other kids fear him. If the boy was cute, Jimmy would sometimes give him a break. Not that it got him anywhere. He'd go home after the game thinking of the boy and wondering why he felt such an attraction. Unlike the missing Harris Rothschild, who seemed to embrace his inner Judy practically from birth.

"About six months ago, Harris started acting out," she said. "Home after college, he was directionless. He'd studied to be an English teacher, which did not please his father. Of course Saul wanted him to be a lawyer. Teachers don't make money, but Harris was insistent, saying what did he need with money? We had enough, and he'd one day inherit it. He was always harping on Saul about how much of an older father he was. But as much as Harris fought to get his degree, once he had it, he chose not to pursue that career track. He spent his days lazing about the house, taking vacations to Europe when the mood struck him, coming home after a night of partying just as Saul was leaving for work, anything but put his education to work." She paused. "A few times he'd get this phone call and disappear into his room to talk. He was secretive and if you asked, forget it. I guess I pushed too hard one night. The next morning I woke up, and he was gone."

"Gone?"

"No note," she said.

"He used to leave notes?"

"All the time. Once his father and I granted him his independence when he reached age twelve, we insisted that he always let us know where he was, or where he was going, who he would be with. Even when he went off to college, he would text us with his plans. Even when he came home, he wrote the notes, but they had taken on a decidedly sarcastic tone, toying with us."

"Asserting himself."

"Only one time did he fail to leave us a note."

"When was this?"

"Two weeks ago," she said.

"And you haven't heard from him since?"

"Not a peep," Jellison Rothschild said. "Don't you find that strange?"

Strange was one word. Angry young man, spreading his wings, testing his sexuality, flying in the face of his parents' expectations. It could be as simple as he had found a lover and they were shacked up somewhere. Or he could be floating in the East River.

"Will you help us?"

"I'll see what I can find out, sure," he said. "I'll need to know much more about him. Can we start with a photograph?"

Jellison rose from the sofa and pulled a gold-leafed frame off the fireplace mantel. She handed it to Jimmy, who studied the face inside the frame. In a word, Harris was beautiful, with classic features so delicate he might have been mistaken for a woman. Perhaps some chromosomes got confused in the womb, which might account for his like of women's shoes, his attraction to men. He had short blond hair and a barely detectable shadow of beard on his cheeks and behind his twinkling blue eyes, Jimmy detected the soul of a poet. Growing up with a high-powered lawyer for a father and a society-obsessed mother, it couldn't have been easy for the only child, expectations being grander than the apartment.

"So, where do you think he's gone?"

She shook her head. "If I knew…"

He nodded, he understood. That's why he was here.

"Saul will handle the financials arrangements," she said. "So if you'll excuse me, I'll see that Saul is getting you the information you require about Harris."

With that, the shapely, sorrowful Jellison Rothschild made her exit, stylish and effective despite the sorrow that struck at her heart. She had to keep up appearances after all, a stiff upper lip and all that. Her face, frozen from Botox injections, had no problem living up to that.

Jimmy was left to his own devices for the first time since arriving, and he took the chance to get up and examine the room a bit further. The way people lived offered up clues as to why someone would want to vacate their premises so unexpectedly, so mysteriously. He strode over to the mantel, where additional photographs were displayed. Harris throughout the years, an infant, a child graduating from middle school, the young man he'd become. It could have been a shrine to a departed relative, and Jimmy had to hope this wasn't the case.

"Ah, Jimmy, there you are," said Saul Rothschild.

"Haven't left," he said.

Rothschild came into the living room, his arm extended. This time it wasn't a handshake he had to offer but a long white envelope. Jimmy accepted it and tucked it into his jacket pocket. A retainer.

"Don't you want to look at it?"

"If I run out, I'll let you know," Jimmy said.

"Spare no expense, Jimmy. Do what you have to, and fear nothing if you find you need to, how shall we say, bend the law to your advantage? Any trouble, you'll have the full backing of my firm. For Jellison's sake, bring our son, Harris, back home..." he said, a strange phrase indeed. Like he couldn't care less. "...alive."

Jimmy couldn't help it. He had to ask the question, and he wasn't guaging the response, but how Rothschild said it. "Mr. Rothschild, is there reason to suspect foul play?"

Even a blind man could have read the fear on the old man's face.

"No," he answered. "But if he got in with the wrong crowd... we have money."

Which meant it could be a kidnapping, the ransom yet to be delivered.

Jimmy found himself staring out the windows at the vastness of Manhattan.

"I'll find him," he said, hoping that was true.

CHAPTER FOUR

The big question when Jimmy was handed a new case was always the same: where to begin?

For Richard Hickney, it started with Jimmy spying on him from across the street of his office building in Lower Manhattan, and whenever he emerged at the end of the day, Jimmy had easily slipped in behind him to follow him to his assignations. The guy was so busy checking the time, he paid no attention to the fact he was being trailed.

For Harris Rothschild, Jimmy had no such obvious jumping off point.

Finding a gay man in New York was like finding hay in a haystack. Didn't mean you'd find the right farm.

As he was leaving the pre-war building at 84th Street, he considered a return subway trip but then voted against it. He needed to ponder his next move and the expanse of Central Park was at his feet. Its winding pathways, thick brush, and persistent joggers and cyclists would be enough to keep him from feeling alone. Turned out, company joined him.

"Mr. McSwain…" someone called out from behind. "Jimmy, wait up."

He'd been about to cross Fifth against the light, that's how minimal the traffic was at two in the afternoon. But he waited until an out-of-breath Jellison Rothschild caught up with him. She was wrapped up in a pink jacket and had slid leather gloves over her manicured hands, her tightly wound blonde hair immovable as she rushed toward him.

"Jellison…" he said, his voice fading after he spoke her name. It was an odd one.

"I'm so glad I caught up with you," she said. "There's more I should tell you."

He nodded. He'd suspected as much, knowing something was

holding her back upstairs.

"Saul oftentimes avoids the details, focusing only on the big picture."

So that was the something. Jimmy said nothing, letting the silence keep her talking.

"He wants his son found, yes, but he doesn't want the particulars."

Jimmy said nothing about the fact that Rothschild suspected foul play.

"Shall we go for a stroll?" she asked. "It's such a lovely afternoon."

Jimmy extended his elbow. The wife Rothschild wrapped her gloved hand around his arm, and the two of them crossed Fifth Avenue. Walking past the Metropolitan Museum of Art, they wound their way into the park at 85th Street, where traffic headed toward the West Side. They took to the path up a hill to the Jacqueline Kennedy Onassis Reservoir. Small talk about the joys of having the park so near her home kept them occupied until they reached the path that circled the reservoir. Then they dug into the matter at hand.

Jimmy took the lead.

"Did Harris have a boyfriend?"

"Not that I'm aware of, but he always tried to keep his personal life...personal."

"Even from you?"

"What does that mean?"

"Mothers and gay sons, sometimes they have a special bond."

"Is that what you have with your mother?"

"I guess so. She's an unstoppable force."

"And your father?"

Jimmy squinted against the harsh sun, his gaze settling upon the rippling waters of the reservoir. "Joseph McSwain, Jr., was a

New York City policeman. He was gunned down one morning while off duty. I was fourteen at the time." He paused, the memory still so fresh, especially at this time of year. "I was there. He died in my arms."

"Oh, Jimmy...I'm...I don't know what to say. 'Sorry' seems so inadequate."

"Lots about my father's death can be qualified as inadequate."

"Did they catch his killer?"

"I'm a private investigator, aren't I?" he stated.

"This case, it's not just a job for you."

"I don't like to see fathers and sons at odds with each other," he said. "And from what I witnessed, Rothschild and Harris had a less than loving relationship. Is it just the gay thing, or is there bad blood that I should know about?"

"Saul's seventy-four. I think he wants a grandchild before he dies."

"Is that happening anytime soon?"

"Which?" she asked.

Jimmy let the enigmatic remark go, focusing on the beauty surrounding them. As they strolled along on the reservoir, joggers passed them, while tourists who spoke in foreign tongues stopped to take pictures of themselves. Central Park was coming alive as spring neared. The trees were not quite budding, but you could sense it coming, the warmth trying to settle in the air. Still, the chill pervaded and Jellison kept her hold on his arm. Jimmy accepted it for what it was, transference. She missed her son.

"Where do you think Harris is? I mean, he could be anywhere in the world."

Jellison shook her head. "He's in New York, I'm sure of it."

"Got any evidence to support that theory?"

"His passport is still in the safe inside the apartment, Saul keeps it under lock."

"Why?"

"Harris has free reign to do as he pleases—to a point."

"Such control could make Harris jealous or angry."

"It's not a new development, their contentious relationship. Saul has expectations and Harris has, in his eyes, met none of them. Harris's sudden disappearance is unrelated to any long instilled issue."

"Then what is it related to?"

She tapped his arm, and he looked up at her. "That's why we've hired you."

This wasn't going to be easy, not when the answers to his questions were as elusive as a criminal on the loose. He was bound to find those answers, not just the surface meanings but what lived beneath them. The real story. Simmering jealousy, angry resentment? It's the typical stuff that tears families apart so often, and toss in the kind of money the Rothschilds had and things could get nasty before they got nice.

Jimmy considered his next question carefully.

"So, no boyfriend. Surely he has a friend. A confidante?"

She pursed her lips, as though trying to keep the answer safely inside. "There's this gentleman."

"Gentleman," Jimmy said, remembering Saul's use of the word "boy" in referencing him. Which told him that "gentleman" meant older. He noted it, nodded.

"His name is Terence."

"Does Terence get a last name?"

"Black," Jellison said.

"Okay, Terence Black, that's a start. What can you tell me about him?"

"He's older, perhaps in his forties or more. I don't know the circumstances behind how they met, only that once they did, he was all Harris could talk about. Terence was this endless source of wisdom. To Harris, he was sliced bread before it had been invented."

"Anything a bit more specific?"

"The night we argued, the night he left…Harris confessed that Terence fed his soul."

"Fed his soul? Curious expression."

To Jimmy, it sounded like love bordering on delusion. To be caught up in a man's world, subscribing to his philosophy. Unless it was some cult he'd run off and joined, one man's "wisdom" could influence your decisions and make you consider doing things you would not normally do. What his hold was on Harris was still to be determined, but at least Jimmy had a starting off point.

By now they had wound their way around the reservoir's perimeter, and they slipped off the path at 90th Street, passing through Engineer's Gate and emerging onto the corner of Fifth. Jellison pressed her hair, as though it had moved. He noticed a tear on her cheek. It could have been from the wind.

"I'll do the best that I can," he offered up as comfort. "If Harris is in New York, I'll find him. Terence Black is as good a place to start as any, I suppose. Uncommon first name, all too common last."

"Thank you, Jimmy. You have a way of making a woman secure."

"Maybe because I'm no threat?"

She smiled. "Too bad, you seem to be quite the catch. What about you? Boyfriend?"

The image of him and the cute Englishman Barry writhing in hot passion on the sofa bed flashed in his mind. Had that occurred only last night, a mere twelve hours ago? He hoped his face didn't betray a mental picture. Jellison patted his arm again.

"It's complicated," he finally said.

"Shame. Handsome man like you. Just the right amount of edge but not cocky."

A joke would be don't tell a gay man he's not cocky. Jimmy let it slide.

He realized they were catching curious looks from other people. A younger man, a not so older woman, he the rough-and-tumble part, she the preserved society lady. Such a pairing wasn't uncommon, and in the middle of the day, too. Hubby hard at work, wifey hard at play. They bypassed a vendor selling hot dogs and hot pretzels, away from the lingering looks. Jimmy pulled his arm away, releasing her grip on him.

"Can I ask you one more question?" he said.

"You can ask. An answer I can't guarantee."

"Your name, Jellison."

She laughed, her sound catching in the delicate wind. "It's a stage name," she said.

"Were you actually on the stage?"

"Two credits, understudy both. But I went on a lot. The leading lady was a bitch."

"What was the show?"

"First one I did was *Cats*. I understudied Grizabella."

"Ah, the glamour cat. She's the character who sings 'Memory.'"

"You surprise me, Jimmy. Not many men would know that reference."

"I am gay," he said. "Aren't I supposed to love Broadway musicals? My mother is also the head usher of a Broadway theatre. I grew up running around the aisles."

"Not the Winter Garden, by chance?"

"No, I never saw you on stage. I'm sure that I would have remembered."

"You're sweet. I was good. Faking comes easy to me."

"And the second show?"

"*Gypsy*. When I started getting old stripper roles, I knew time was running out on finding my sugar daddy."

He took note of that. "What's your real name?"

"Myrna Clary." She paused, her hand covering her mouth. "I

can't believe I said that."

"Parents can be cruel," he said.

"Not just at birth," she remarked.

It was another curious comment whose words faded away even if their impact didn't, and Jimmy filed it away for another time. He just knew he wasn't getting the whole story about the relationship between father and son, much less mother and son. Why hire a private investigator when you weren't going to be forthcoming with details? Like a twist on the old military ban on gays, ask but don't tell.

They parted near the Guggenheim, Jellison striding forward at a decent clip, Pilates on cement. Jimmy remained behind, going back to the sidewalk vendor and scarfing down a hot dog with mustard and tart sauerkraut. It was a far cry from the decadent food he'd consumed at lunch, but it was just as tasty, maybe more so, because even in this rarefied world of Museum Mile, he felt like he was almost home.

He decided that was just where he wanted to be.

He walked it, back through the park. Why not? It was a nice day.

He might not be able to say the same thing about the upcoming nights.

Because he had a feeling finding Harris Rothschild would be done in the dark of night.

§ § §

He arrived back home at five-thirty to find his mother packing to go to the theatre for the night. Tuesday night on Broadway meant early curtain, seven p.m., which meant she had to be there at six. He was coming up the stairs when she opened the door to the apartment.

"Oh, Jimmy, there you are."

"Been working, Ma."

"And now it's time for me to work. Walk with me."

For the second time today, a woman wrapped her arms around him. They walked along 48th Street until they came to Ninth, then followed the lights until crossing at 47th. The Harold Calloway Theatre was between 8th and Broadway, another long block until they reached their destination. He and Maggie engaged in normal chitchat, he telling her he fell asleep at his office last night while working on the case file, she nodding, either oblivious to the truth or not wanting to know. She was like that, Jimmy knew. She chose her moments when to pry into his personal life. They walked slowly, Maggie claiming her knee was barking at her because those fool ushers who worked in the balcony had made her trudge up all those steps to make sure they had enough *Playbills*.

"Why can't they do it themselves? They're working up there."

"Because they're fools, useless as the flight of steps are long."

The now-landmarked Harold Calloway Theatre had been built in 1928, a year before Wall Street crashed. Calloway himself had been a celebrated theatre actor who'd not only made shrewd investments that enabled him to have a theater constructed, but he'd long seen his rival, the Ethel Barrymore Theatre down the street, enjoy great success, its namesake winning prizes and acclaim. So he bought the lot next door and built it, starring in several productions in his own theatre, only to die in his dressing room on the final night of his less-than-well-received turn in *Hamlet*. Legend had it that Calloway was so annoyed with his critics that he chose death over ever returning to the stage. It is said his ghost still haunts the place.

For now, though, the front of the house belonged to Maggie McSwain, and the assembled staff grew silent as she arrived, waiting for instructions from their chief about what aisles to work. Jimmy hung around, watching as the orchestra ushers set up large stacks of *Playbills* on their aisles, listening to them gripe about one of their regulars who had taken off her late shift again. It was a common litany, complaining about what others did, or he supposed, in his case, didn't do.

As he wandered the orchestra level, staring at the ceiling

adorned with Tiffany lights and stained glass, he drifted back to his childhood. When his father was on his beat, busy at night on the streets of New York, Jimmy and Mallory and eventually Meaghan could be found running up and down the aisles before the theatre opened its doors for patrons. For most people, entering a Broadway theatre was to be taken into a magical world of song and dance, of fantasy, of the Janus masks of drama and comedy. For Jimmy McSwain and his sisters and pretty much half of Hell's Kitchen, it was just another playground on the West Side.

He stole a look at the set, a living room in an apartment decorated not unlike the one he'd seen earlier today; the show was a sparkling revival of *You Can't Take It With You* and had been playing to packed houses since its opening in early December. Thanks to a star turn by Kelsey Grammar, ticket sales were healthy, and the show was enjoying an extended run into the spring season. Jimmy had seen the show on opening night and a few times during the holidays when Maggie was short-staffed. Ushering wasn't his favorite job, but he did it when needed. It was good pocket money.

Turned out tonight was going to be one of those times.

"Jimmy, Helen just called. Her subway is delayed, she's not going to make it."

Looking at his sister Meaghan, who worked on one of the center orchestra aisles, he mouthed the word "Help."

"Yeah, like you ever say no to Ma."

Jimmy always kept a change of clothes in a locker downstairs in the usher's room. Before he could protest, his mother informed him he was working aisle four in the orchestra, so he went downstairs and changed into the Calloway uniform of black shirt, black pants, and a red tie with a scripted "C." Most of the theatres, like the seventeen owned by the Shubert Organization, had men wearing white shirts, but they didn't always look so crisp or fresh. The black-on-black was a sleeker look. Soon, Jimmy was dressed and on his aisle, setting up his *Playbills*, checking his flashlight, and wishing his mother hadn't asked him to work.

Didn't he have a case to investigate? He was set to go, though, and a few minutes later the manager announced, "The house is open." For the next thirty minutes, patrons arrived and the ushering crew sat them, handing out *Playbills* and telling them to enjoy the show and please, turn off your cell phones, a plea that fell on deaf ears. That is, until their phone inevitably rang during the show; that they heard, and so did the actors.

Jimmy was told he would be on the late shift tonight, and with the show running longer than two and a half hours, it meant he wasn't getting out until nearly ten o'clock. During Act One, he was sent to the balcony to relieve the usher up there, and his mind wandered as he sat in the dark. He thought about the day just passed: waking up in the arms of Barry, a parting kiss promising they would get together again; his journey to Fifth Avenue and the luncheon with the Rothschilds, their concern over missing son Harris; the talk with Jellison while they circled the Central Park reservoir.

Jellison Rothschild was an enigma. A caring mother concerned about her son, but also a society lady who specialized in lunches with ladies of similar social status. Yet she had a past spent upon the so-called wicked stage, and now, as he stared at the actors cavorting upon the Calloway stage, he considered the idea that today's luncheon had been just as staged. His sister Mallory hadn't needed to be there, but her presence had helped set Jimmy at ease. Was that deliberate on Rothschild's part? No doubt. Had his talk with Jellison been orchestrated as well? Had Saul sent her chasing after him, a director shaping his actor's performance? And what of this mystery character Terence Black? Why had Jellison planted this seed? A red herring or an important turning point in the plot?

Unlike the drama on the stage that would end with a neat resolution, all of Jimmy's questions went unanswered. The night progressed, and with it the show. Before long it was over. Suddenly applause filled the house, and bows were taken. The house lights came up.

Jimmy cleared his aisle and helped close the front doors as the last of the patrons departed.

Maggie had been on late as well, so they walked home together, a reverse of what they'd done just hours ago. Meaghan had been on the early shift, so she'd left after flash-off, ten minutes into the show. Jimmy and his mother were arm-in-arm again, her talking a mile a minute about the events of the night, a story of a customer complaining the house was too cold.

"We had a house of eight hundred twelve tonight, so how do you adjust the temperature for one person? Don't know why people don't get that. It's three hours of your life. If that's the worst thing to happen to you, shut up and don't question God's plan."

Jimmy smiled at her. He'd been hearing these complaints for years. Nothing changed because people never changed.

Everyone was out for themselves. It was all about their comfort, their motives.

Was the same true of the Rothschilds?

Jimmy convinced his mother to join him at Paddy's, so they ambled their way along Ninth Avenue, stepping past a group of smokers outside and into the noisy dankness of the dive bar. Paddy was, of course, behind the bar, but when he saw Maggie, he came around and kissed her cheek, pulling out a bar stool for his sister. She hoisted herself up and ordered a martini "with gin, like you're supposed to."

"For you, Maggie McDear, how else would it be made?" Paddy said.

Jimmy had a Guinness.

Drinks poured, stools occupied, Maggie thanked him for filling in.

"No problem, Ma. For you, anytime."

"You put in a long day. How was your meeting?"

"I got a job, if that's what you're asking."

"Mallory knows some important people."

"Important people would refer to the people I met as important."

"That good?"

"My retainer pays for my office for the next year."

Maggie leaned over to sip at her full glass. Lifting it might waste a few precious drops.

"What's the case?"

"I'd rather not get into it," he said.

Maggie nodded. "You keep things bottled in too much, Jimmy."

"Ma…"

"What? You do. Someday, Jimmy, you're gonna have to find happiness."

"I'm happy."

She waved a dismissive hand. "You ever hear from Remy?"

Why was she going there? Jimmy felt a stab at his heart, drank his stout. Thick as it was, it didn't seal the wound.

Fortunately, his cell phone rang and broke the chain of their conversation. He didn't recognize the number flashing on the lit screen, but if it meant not talking about Remy with his mother—hell, with anyone—he would have taken a collect call from the Devil.

"This is Jimmy."

"This is Barry."

"Oh, hey, hi."

"Bad time?"

Jimmy looked at his mother, who was looking back at him. He excused himself and felt her curious gaze follow him as he went outside. It wasn't any less noisy on the sidewalk than it was inside the pub, what with taxi horns and some jerk yelling out "Yo, Adrian," which was probably just some drunk idiot with a *Rocky* fixation.

"Better time now," Jimmy said into the phone.

"I just wanted to call…and, well, didn't want to be needy, but also…"

"It's okay, Barry. Good to hear your voice."

"I had a good time last night, totally unexpected meeting someone. Meeting you."

"I did too. And yeah, I wasn't expecting to meet anyone either."

"So, do you want to get together, you know, sometime?"

"Pretty ambiguous, sometime."

"Friday night," he said.

"That's more specific, I like that. Yeah, sure. A date, or you just want to come over?"

"No, a date. A real one. I'll come up with something fun. Or you can. First one with the idea wins."

"Done."

They said goodnight and when the call was silenced, Jimmy stared at the phone.

"Huh," he said, trying to decide whether he was excited or frightened.

Resuming his seat and taking a larger pull of his Guinness, he tried to avoid his mother's stare. It wasn't easy. . It was almost as though the rest of bar had grown more quiet, perhaps everyone else wanting to know his business.

"What?"

"So," she said, "What's his name?"

Some mothers, they knew their sons frontwards, backwards, forwards, and even further, deep into their hearts.

And then there was Jellison Rothschild.

CHAPTER FIVE

Private eyes of yesteryear had their wits to rely on, their street smarts.

It's what made them successful.

Today, the rules had all changed. Today you had Google search.

Jimmy was home, thankfully alone, on what turned out to be a damp, rainy Wednesday afternoon. The Calloway had a two-show day, so his mother and Meaghan had gone off to work. Jimmy, lounging in shorts and a T-shirt, showered but remained unshaven. He grabbed a second cup of coffee, sat down at the desktop computer in his bedroom, and typed in the words "Terence Black." What he got back was of no help at all, since there were too many people with that name, some of them white, some black, a few of them offering up LinkedIn profiles, Twitter accounts, and invitations to become friends on Facebook. He clicked the links in an effort to gain insight, clues, anything that might send him down a path that led to the Terence Black he sought. In the end, results were inconclusive and Jimmy, sipping at his coffee, his eyes tired from the harsh glow of the screen, considered his next move. Just using the man's name wasn't proving to be enough to go on, so Jimmy had to narrow his search. There was one obvious word to use, and so he added the word "gay."

That narrowed things down a bit, but still not enough. He ended up with results of people named Terence Gay, one of whom shared an article in which he was the victim of a beating and was quoted as saying he'd received a "black" eye. Google sometimes went a bit broad in their key words, so Jimmy had to rethink his approach.

Getting up from his chair, he made his way into the kitchen and poured a fresh cup of joe.

Pacing the apartment, he eventually opened up the curtains

and stared out at the messy, rainy streets of Manhattan. He could be out there, pounding the pavement, seeking out Harris Rothschild in places where gay men were known to hang out. But it was still too early for the nocturnal creatures to emerge, and Jimmy had a sense that's when Harris liked to play. No doubt they slept now, wasting the day away until it was time to waste the night.

He went back to work, sifting through the various items Jellison had given him.

First, he stared at the photograph of the beautiful Harris, with his high cheekbones that would be the envy of most women. Second, he flipped through the paperwork from Rothschild, including a copy of his passport. The last place he'd gone outside of the country was Paris, in January. He wondered if Harris had gone alone, and again the question came up about whether the guy had a boyfriend. He seemed to be a private man, sure of his sense of self but unsure in the presence of his parents. Like he was two men.

Wouldn't that be an easy solution to the case of Where's Harris? He and his hot flame on a two-week bender of sex, drugs, and rock and roll, or whatever music they liked. The point was, Harris could have tired of his parents' endless attempts at control and run off to indulge whatever he felt was lacking in his life. Maybe this Terence Black was his lover after all, even if he was older. Harris had been around an older father his entire life, and Jimmy had to imagine Saul Rothschild was not an easy man to please. Toss in the gay angle, and you had the makings of conflict.

What he visualized suddenly was not Harris, but Saul, witnessing his young son prancing around in high heels. Firmly telling the pretty boy to put those ridiculous shoes back, let's go to the park and toss around a baseball. Forcing stereotypical displays of masculinity down his throat when he all he wanted to do was play dress up and break out into song. For Harris Rothschild, growing up must have been a drag. He thought again of the shoes.

Light bulbs sometimes go off when you least expect them, infusing a once rainy day with a glow of discovery. Now was one of those times.

Energized, Jimmy returned to the computer and narrowed his search even further.

Terence. Black. Gay. Drag.

And a website address popped up immediately. The Dress Up Club.

One click later, he had landed on the home page, not sure what to expect but ready for anything. The club could be found in Chelsea, at Tenth Avenue and Twenty-Second Street, and from the photographs provided, it specialized in drag performances. Gay men dolled up in whatever pop culture icon they idolized, or for some just a creation of their own. Jimmy saw several photos of one man in particular, the caption stating, "Your host Terry Cloth will welcome you with open arms."

Experience had taught Jimmy to assume that Terry Cloth was none other than Terence Black.

Even though he was convinced he had found the right person, he surveyed the remainder of the site, clicking on About Us. Contact Us, and Upcoming Events, and something called Outreach. The latter button intrigued him the most, so he clicked on it, only to have a page load that read: "This page under construction."

Not very outreach-y of them.

Jimmy next went to Upcoming Events, which provided a calendar of the club's featured performers. They didn't perform drag shows every night; some nights they offered up a regular cabaret with lounge singers, Broadway performers, and amateur night on Wednesdays. But the big appeal seemed to be the drag shows, which played on Tuesdays, Fridays, and Saturdays. He'd just missed last night's show, which had featured a six-foot-four performer in a shapely devil's outfit, with the clever name of Hell on Heels. It had been billed as "One Night Only."

But on Wednesday nights, like tonight, as the schedule noted, the club allowed amateurs to perform, leaving Jimmy wondering how much advance notice was required to take to the glittery stage. Did you show up unannounced and take the mic? Did you need to call ahead? Jimmy clicked on the Contact Us button, coming up with a general email address for info@dressupclub. com, followed by a phone number. You could also sign up for their monthly newsletter and receive periodic weekly updates for their events.

Jimmy didn't feel like emailing. Who knew who would see it and when?

Calling was an option, but that might tip his hand.

If Terence Black was indeed such a good friend of Harris Rothschild's, chances were he might know where the young heir was hiding out. Chances were, too, if Harris didn't want to be found, good old Terry Cloth would do his best to hide him, perhaps in the voluminous material of a huge white robe Terry was often photographed wearing. Nope, a phone call wouldn't do. Jimmy liked to read faces, interpret body language, no matter how they were dressed. Most people's poker faces sucked. They would fold at the first sign of trouble.

He had a feeling, though, that Terry Cloth would be a cool customer.

Jimmy turned off the computer and drained the last of his coffee.

Rain notwithstanding, it was time to hit the streets.

He dressed in his usual attire of jeans and black boots, a button-down shirt, and he grabbed his leather jacket before locking up. As Jimmy stepped out into the raw, rainy day a few minutes later, he hailed a passing cab, feeling lucky to get one despite the incessant downpour. But traffic was a mess going down Ninth Avenue, so Jimmy settled against the backseat, knowing that each click of the cab's meter was money on the Rothschild's sizable clock. He was grateful for the time, as it gave him a chance to consider his approach.

Just because he was headed into a den of drag queens, that

didn't mean he shouldn't approach without caution. He'd caught a few acts in his time. Their pointed barbs could scar just as deeply as a thug's fist.

§ § §

The Dress Up Club was closed, its neon sign dark above a rolled-up awning. A placard on the door indicated they opened for Happy Hour at five. It was only two seventeen, Jimmy noted. As rain dripped on him from the sign above, he peered through the front glass, looking for any signs of life inside but seeing only the condensation of his own breath cloud his view. He wiped it away and saw a row of bar stools turned upside down, their legs pointed toward the ceiling. The tables were without linen, lights were off, and a bucket and mop stood unattended in the middle of the room.

Jimmy thought about leaving and coming back at opening but changed his mind as he considered the fact that no one left a dirty wet mop out overnight.

Someone had to be inside.

He knocked on the glass, his knuckles rapping loudly.

No response, so he tried again.

He waited, not so much patient as determined. Rain continued to pelt him, drenching his coat, flattening his hair. He hadn't thought to bring an umbrella. What kind of private eye would he be, afraid of a little rain? At last, a shadow moved inside the establishment. Jimmy knocked again as he saw the shadow take shape. A man of approximately fifty years of age appeared, baldheaded and wearing thick, round glasses. He had a slightly paunchy frame wrapped in a flowing caftan, and he was waving his finger like a dismissive headmistress.

"We're closed," he said from the other side of the glass.

"Yes, I see that," Jimmy said.

"Open at five."

"I can read, too. I'm not interested in a drink."

That comment made the man pause, perhaps understanding

this wasn't a social call.

"Is there something I can do for you, then?"

"You could open the door and let me in."

"Who are you?"

Jimmy, already wet from the rain, didn't mind jumping into the deep end. "I'm a friend of Harris Rothschild."

The man hesitated, as though prepared to say he had no idea who that was.

Instead, he turned the lock and opened the door cautiously.

"I don't know where he is," the man said.

"Terence Black?"

"For the moment," he said, resignation evident on his face. If Jimmy already knew his name, it meant he had the man at a distinct disadvantage. "And who, may I ask, are you? Harris never mentioned he had…a friend. Though I must say he does have good taste. Come in. My goodness, you're soaked. Perhaps we should get you out of those clothes." Those last words more invitation than suggestion.

"Nice try. I'm fine. Just a little wet."

"Surely you couldn't have left your home without an umbrella. It's not like the unsettled weather caught us suddenly unaware. It's been raining buckets since dawn."

"I took a cab," Jimmy said.

"Oh, Mr. Money Bags. Still, didn't do you much good once you got out."

"I can handle a bit of rain."

"At least I know you're not the Wicked Witch," Terence said, a widened smile crossing his face, dark brown pupils widening behind those thick lenses. "So, a tough guy. I like that. A lot."

Jimmy pulled two stools off the bar and set them upright. He sat on one before indicating Terence should do the same.

"Oh, pooh, and I thought you were going to be fun. Down to

business, huh? Whatever is this about?"

"Like I said, it's about Harris."

But Terence didn't sit. Instead he went around the bar and searched out a fresh towel, which he then tossed Jimmy's way. "Dry off while I fetch us something to beverage on."

Beverage on? Was he really using that as a verb?

Terence swung back around the edge of the silver bar, two glasses in hand, a bottle of white wine in the other. Jimmy noticed the man's walk had taken a decidedly swishier gait. The gown trailed behind him, as though wind blown.

"Can I ask what is that you're wearing?"

"It's a caftan, dear. So comfortable, I feel like I'm floating on air when I wear it."

"That part of the show? Is that what it's made of? Terry cloth?"

"Hmm, you are a well-informed young man. Seems you know too much, and I know too little."

"You put stuff up online, people are going to find it."

"And what will I find when I look you up?"

"The only footprints of mine you'll find are at the corner of Tenth Avenue and Forty-eighth. I stepped into fresh cement when the city replaced the sidewalk."

Terence smiled at the comment but said nothing. He poured two glasses of wine. Jimmy wasn't much of a wine drinker, but he drank it to be sociable. He'd already gotten further with this conversation than he'd expected. Was this Terence guy as hospitable as he seemed, or was Jimmy being set up for some kind of sneak attack? Jimmy peered around the man, looking toward the back of the narrow club.

"We're alone, if that's what you're wondering."

"Just checking the place out, never been here before."

"Oh, is a drag club not your kind of place?"

"Guess I don't get it," he said.

"Too bad. I'd love to get you up on our stage, see what untapped talents you've got," Terence said, cocking his head to one side as though picturing Jimmy in full drag. "Course for a true drag experience, we'd have to do some work on you. Send you to the spa for a good waxing."

"Excuse me?"

"You're the rough and tumble type, so we'd need to give you a bit of makeover. Hard not to notice that bear rug sprouting up out of your wet shirt," Terence said, eyeing Jimmy's open-collared shirt. "I could knit sweaters for kittens with that yummy fur."

"Kittens have their own, I'll keep mine, too."

Terence expressed a look of dismay. "Boo. Thought you were a tough guy. Nothing like a waxing to test your pain level. So, Mr. Sexy Stranger, what I can do for you today? Perhaps we could start with your name?"

"Call me Jimmy."

"Jimmy. You can call me intrigued."

"Intrigued."

Terence allowed himself a chuckle, the tone clear he didn't mean it.

"And how do you know Harris?"

"Want the truth?"

"Even if you say you're telling the truth, how do I know it is?"

Good point. Jimmy pulled his wallet out, showed his investigator's license. With a hand clasped against his chest, Terence let out a mock squeal. "Why, a real life private eye is sitting right here at my humble Dress Up Club. This is getting much more interesting. Let me guess, those clueless dolts who call themselves Harris's parents hired you to find him."

"How do you know he's missing?"

Terence took his wine glass in hand, raised his pinky, and

said, his voice finding a higher, snooty register, "Our precious son Harris, he's just going through an awkward phase. He didn't mean to buy that lovely blouse the other day. He'll come to realize it's not the lifestyle he wants, he'll outgrow it and soon he'll be visiting his repressed wife at night and producing heirs, one, two, perhaps three.'" He paused, drank some wine. "How'd I do?"

"Jellison's not English," Jimmy said.

"God, that name. Such a fabrication. No wonder she's got a gay son."

"Jellison also doesn't seem to have a problem with that. Saul on the other hand…"

"Look, Jimmy, you're a total hottie, and I'd love to help you. But if Harris doesn't want to see his parents, that's his call. He's a grown man…except when he's not. Now, if you wouldn't mind, I have tons of work to do before we open and Clara Bell, my usual bartender, is down with the flu so I've gotta open until relief shows up."

Jimmy had gotten more info than he'd expected and decided he should leave and digest what, he'd learned. Perhaps there were additional clues buried in there somewhere.

Rising from his seat, he slid his business card beneath the stem of his wine glass. "You see Harris, tell him he can contact me. Or more simply, just tell him to call home and let his worried parents know nothing untoward has happened to him."

"Untoward. Fancy word. Like something Harris would say."

"So long as Harris doesn't have to experience something bad happening to him."

"Is that what you think, that Harris being here is bad for him?"

"You tell me."

"Going home, that would be the worst for him. They've already broken him."

"You got super glue here, putting Humpty Dumpty back together again?"

"He's already got a different identity."

Jimmy wasn't sure how to interpret that. Instead, he just said, "Tell E.T. to phone home."

"No guarantee, Jimmy."

"Just like life," he remarked.

As Jimmy made his way toward the front door, he turned back.

"You change your mind about the spa treatment?"

"Uh, no. Just wondering something. The name of your club, I find it rather curious. From what I've heard about drag queens, they don't consider what they do as dressing up. Not like mama's closet back home. What they're doing goes beyond serious craft, filling up something they're missing. You know," he paused, tapping his chest, "in here."

"Oh, don't take it so literally, Jimmy. It's about much more than simply dressing up."

Jimmy waited for the punch line he could see forming on Terence's lips.

"Lift the dress up, you'll be surprised by what you see underneath."

Jimmy actually laughed. "Nicely played, Terry Cloth. Have a good one. And like I said, tell Harris to reach out, let us know he's not in any trouble."

Before he could leave, it was Terence who stopped him this time. He turned, not ready to face the rain anyway. "You should come see our show sometime."

Jimmy wondered if the invitation was as innocent as it appeared.

Or was there an agenda behind it? A clue that would lead him to Harris.

"Sure, how about Friday," he said.

"I'll pencil you in. The ten o'clock show is usually more fun than the earlier one."

"Good, make the reservation for two," Jimmy said. "I'll bring my new boyfriend."

He departed then to the sound of Terence's laughter, only to have the pouring rain drown it out immediately. No cabs were available this time, so Jimmy started walking up Tenth Avenue. When he turned back, he looked at not just the front façade of the Dress Up Club, but at the building itself and the apartments above it. What caught his attention was the flash of yellow light against the dark sky, and a face in the window of the apartment right above the club. But then it was gone, shielded by a curtain falling into place.

He wouldn't swear on it in court, but he thought the face belonged to a woman.

CHAPTER SIX

Jimmy wished he could avoid moments like this. Phone calls were good, emails were better. Just "click" send, let cyberspace do its thing and voila, the case was over. Wait for the check to arrive, deposit it, move on. But one client just wouldn't let it go, so that's how he found himself face-to-face with her at the Moonstruck diner at Ninth Avenue and 23rd Street at two in the afternoon on Thursday, witnessing the pain on his client's face and the devastation in her heart. Half-eaten burgers remained between them, as did a plate of fries that so far had only been picked at. Ketchup made him think of blood.

"Mrs. Hickney...."

"Please, call me Sissy."

He had a hard time with that one, considering he'd outed her husband.

"Fine, Sissy. So, how's your week gone? I'm guessing you've had better."

"Awful, fine, great, horrible," she said.

Emotions ping-ponging inside her, doing their damage. "And your husband?"

"Oh, he's still at home, called in sick the rest of the week."

"So you didn't kick him out." A statement, not a question.

"What, and let him take a room in Manhattan, and do... whomever?"

She had a point, and Jimmy nodded. "What are your options?"

Sissy Hickney looked like she hadn't slept since receiving Jimmy's report, as though the very question of what her future held had kept her up at nights. A week ago she was a pretty, curly-haired blonde, but now her hair lacked sheen, her face looked drained, devoid of make-up, and rings settled under her eyes. She'd been through the wringer, and the way she was picking at the French fries that sat between them, he was worried she wasn't taking care of herself. People all react differently to crisis. Some triumph, some wallow in misery, some curl up and allow their souls to be destroyed.

"He stays put, he behaves like a father should, end of story."

Jimmy hoped she understood her solution really wasn't a solution and perhaps she wasn't ready to face the truth. He knew her actions were for the sake of their son, but what damage would it do to him, to her, in the long term? He often wondered if his father were still around, how different would his life be? Would he have pursued the private eye route, or would he have enrolled in the police academy and now be patrolling the mean streets as a second-generation cop? If his father had continued to take him to Mets games, if his father had showed him how to drive a car, to work a drill set, a wrench, how might that have changed him? What he was questioning was his moral center, his inner strength, his fortitude when it came to looking out for his sisters and mother. If Joseph McSwain, Jr. still graced their dinner table all these years, Jimmy wouldn't have had to step up so much to look out for his family.

From what he'd seen, he doubted Richard Hickney was up to the task of looking after his own family.

"What happens to the marriage?" Jimmy asked.

"How do you mean? It's over…it exists in name only."

"Where does Richard sleep?"

"By himself," she said. "In the guest bedroom."

"And your son? What do you tell him?"

"Dad's not feeling well. That's what we've gone with."

"Dads get better," Jimmy advised, thinking unless of course they die. "But I'm no marriage counselor. I'm just a hired gun and not a good one, since I don't carry a gun."

"A private investigator without a gun?"

Jimmy held up his hands. "I use these. Hopefully my wits first."

"Yes, I saw the result of those fists," she said, a slight smile cracking through her sorrow. "Thank you. I'm sure he deserved it."

"He clocked me first," Jimmy said.

"Really, Rich was…violent?"

Jimmy wished he hadn't said anything. Now he was just putting ideas in her head. Fears.

"He was provoked…"

"Oh, and living inside your home as a prisoner isn't provoking him?"

"Like I said, I'm not a counselor." He'd left off the word "marriage" this time. The problem probably went deeper than just issues of intimacy, of love. Trust had been breached, and often what previously existed between two people couldn't be rebuilt. And from all Sissy was saying, she didn't even want to attempt to patch things up. He didn't blame her. How could she when her husband wanted to prowl gay bars and pick up men?

"So, Sissy, you wanted to meet with me, in the city. Why?"

"Could you take me to, you know…where you found him?"

"I don't think that's such a good idea. You've got the photographs, isn't that enough?"

"We met in college," she said, "and I thought he was the most handsome man ever. We hit it off, English lit, *Romeo and Juliet.* Isn't that a laugh now? I should have known we were doomed. But no, I fell in love with him, and I thought he fell in love with me. Sometimes…it was odd, we'd be out with friends and I'd see him staring forward, not listening, like the empty space in front of him was more interesting than his friends…than me. What did I know then? I was barely nineteen and in the thralls of my first major love affair. He was so patient with me, waiting nearly six months before we…you know…"

Jimmy nodded. She remained the proper, put-upon New Jersey housewife. You didn't discuss sex with anyone, even the man you hired to find evidence of your husband's cheating ways with other men.

"Anyway, he dazzled me, and I knew I'd met the most perfect man. My parents, oh how they adored him, and his parents were over the moon for me. We dated all through college, got married a year after graduation. He didn't want to have a family right away, he needed to launch his career. I played along, took a part-time job at a women's-only gym, stayed in shape. When Aidan came along, I thought we had everything. Rich was the doting father and husband, and I began to believe the sun shined extra bright on us."

Jimmy was growing restless, shifting in his seat. He didn't know what their life story had to do with seeking a visit to Slings & Arrows. He wanted to prod her along, but instead stuffed a fry into his mouth. He chewed as he listened.

"I'm sorry, I know this is the long version of what's become a short story. Jimmy, I want to go to that bar because of the photographs—especially the ones of Rich sitting alone at the bar. He has that look in his eyes, the one I used to see when we'd go out to dinner. He wasn't lost in his own world. He was just scoping out the place. Maybe even back then he was looking for hook-ups."

Jimmy nodded and set down the last fry.

"It's not too far from here," he said.

"I know. I chose this location for a reason. I was going with or without you."

"With me is the better option," he said.

Her smile was genuine, maybe for the first time since arriving.

She insisted on paying the bill, and Jimmy didn't argue. They were soon back outside in the bright sun of an early spring day. They turned down Ninth Avenue and walked with growing anxiety toward the small streets of the West Village. He could see her clenching her fists. Harried people bypassed them, swishing around them with attitude and speed, like their destination was not only more important, but would disappear if they didn't get to it quickly enough. It felt like the world was going at two speeds, heightening his sense of something being…off. Even his shadow was feeling skittish about this venture.

"I don't know how you live in this city," Sissy said. "It's so frenetic."

"I don't know any different," he replied. "Big houses and yards scare me."

"I don't think much scares you, Jimmy McSwain."

Death does. Being alone does. He closed his eyes, and the world seemed brighter when he reopened them.

They made their way to the bar on Christopher Street, where Jimmy led her down three steps. Opening wide the wooden door, they went inside the dark basement-level bar. Unlike the Dress Up Club, whose primary business was cabaret entertainment fueled by the nightlife, Slings & Arrows rarely closed. You wanted a beer at eight in the morning, you went here. You wanted companionship with that beer, you could get that. You wanted to be left alone, you shield your eyes and don't scope. Despite its seedy look, streaks of bright light filtered in through small windows near the ceiling, offering up a slight ray of hope.

"Charming place," Sissy said.

"Seen enough?"

"Not yet," she said, approaching the bar.

A man covered with tattoos that peeked out beneath his wife-beater stared at them.

"You sure you're in the right place, honey?"

"She's okay, Alex," Jimmy said.

"Oh, hey, Jim. You going kinky on us, or is she…?"

"Consider it an underground tour of Manhattan."

He nodded. "We are that. What can I get you?"

Sissy looked at Jimmy, and then back at Alex. "Oh, no…no, nothing for me. Do you mind if I sit at the bar for a moment?"

"Take a load off. How about you, Jim? Beer?"

"Not this time, thanks."

Jimmy sat next to her, watching her surveying the place. A few older men sat at the bar, nursing drinks, eyes curious to see what was transpiring. Middle-aged suburban women coming to Slings & Arrows was practically unheard of. It wasn't even a place the fag hags patronized. This place had been around since the seventies, existing solely as a drinks and pick-up joint. Sissy scanned the room, her eyes landing on the narrow staircase that led down to a further basement. She had read his report. He had informed her what kinds of activities went on down there. A hand went to her mouth, and she turned to Jimmy.

"Rich went...oh God."

"The photos don't do it justice, do they?"

She turned back and signaled the tattooed Alex. "Do you have tequila? A shot."

"This is a bar," he said, "even got lime and salt."

Alex grabbed a bottle and poured her a shot. He set it down in front of her, a dare on his face.

She didn't hesitate. "This isn't a party," she said, knocking the proffered shot back with vigor.

Jimmy accepted one as well and mirrored Sissy's actions.

Alex stood before them with the bottle poised. She shook her head.

"Feel better?" Jimmy asked.

"Get me out of here," she said.

Back outside, she exhaled. "How much do I owe you for today?"

"You bought lunch, you bought the shot. Let's call it even."

She shook her head. "Why couldn't I have met a nice guy like you?"

He didn't feel it was appropriate at this moment to remind her that he, too, was gay.

§ § §

Sissy said she would take the Path train from Christopher Street back to Hoboken where she'd parked the family SUV, returning to the world she once thought safe. As for Jimmy, he'd had enough of the West Village to last him a few weeks, and he'd be back in Chelsea for the Dress Up Club's drag show in one day. His mother didn't need him at the Calloway tonight, at least, not so far. But he kept his cell phone on, ringer on high, just in case.

So, with one case seemingly finished and the other on hold, Jimmy was, for the moment, free.

He went down the stairs at the Sheridan Square subway station, taking the #1 train. He surprised himself by going downtown, and when they hit Canal Street, he hopped off and waited on the platform for either a 2 or 3. It was the 3 to show up first, which he rode through the rest of Manhattan and into the deep tunnels under the East River, finally emerging at the Clark Street station in Brooklyn. This was one of those stations that were built so far underground, riders had to take an elevator to get topside. Which is what he did, journeying upwards with a dozen other people. It was mid-day still, most everyone still at work. Through the turnstile he went, having to then walk through the dingy lobby of the now-defunct Hotel St. George, finally able to breath fresh air again. He slipped on a pair of sunglasses and began to walk along Clark Street a few blocks to Montague Street, the main business thoroughfare in Brooklyn Heights.

He made his way toward an Irish pub named Eamonn's. As he grabbed the door handle, it didn't escape him that his life this week had consisted of hopping from bar to bar, and now he was even doing it in another borough. This one was different from Paddy's, and it sure as hell wasn't Gaslight. This was a typical neighborhood pub with food, where the regulars could sidle up to the bar at any hour and order a beer and a burger. He took a seat and ordered a Smithwicks. At the sound of his voice, the man at the stool next to him spun around and faced him.

"Afternoon, Jim," he said.

"Hi ya, Ralphie."

"Thought I might be seeing you soon," he said, his eyes crinkling behind glasses. Ralphie had dark black skin and a shock of wiry, gray hair. A bit of gray scruff grew on his chin.

Jimmy nodded and drank the foam off the top of his brew. "That time of year."

"St. Patrick's."

"Day after St. Patrick's," he said.

"I remember."

"So do I," Jimmy said, his throat tight. "Fifteen years."

A simple nod, then the man drained the remnants of his glass. "Finish that beer, Jim, let's go for a walk. Nice day out, my legs could use it."

If nothing else, Jimmy was a man of purpose and determination. Beers came and went, but moments of truth were rare. He left the glass half-empty, feeling almost as though he had left the rest in honor of Joseph McSwain, Jr., who'd never tasted a Smithwicks because fifteen years ago the Guinness Company had been unable to export it to the States. Holding open the door, he let Ralphie exit first, aided by a wooden cane topped with a brass-winged eagle.

Ralphie Henderson had been his father's partner, senior in both experience and age. He'd retired with full pension after thirty years. Never been shot at, never fired his gun. He'd been one of the lucky ones, but he'd attended too many cop funerals, seen too much of the wrong side of the law, so he spent many of his days just where Jimmy had found him, either forgetting about his old life or ruminating on how much energy humans expended on being felonious.

"You look good, Ralphie."

"Yeah, seventy is the new forty, right?"

"Where we headed?"

"Promenade, we'll take a seat there."

So they ambled along Montague Street, finally emerging into a more residential area, slipping through a small tree-lined park and onto the wide promenade that lined the edge of Brooklyn Heights. The jagged skyline of Lower Manhattan loomed across the river, glistening in the bright sun. Even though the majestic steel and glass Freedom Tower was near completion, the city still felt like its soul had a large hole in it. Ralphie took a seat on a park bench, Jimmy sitting down next to him.

Joggers went by them, dogs on leashes yapping at their ankles.

"Don't know where they get the energy," Ralphie said.

"The dogs or the joggers?"

"Hmmph. Both." He paused, adjusting his glasses. "How's Maggie?"

"She's good. Asks about you all the time."

"A visit wouldn't hurt," he said, sounding like a man thinking back in time.

"You know her, she doesn't cross state lines."

Ralphie grinned, the lines on his face widening. "Sisters?"

"Everyone's doing great."

"How about you?"

"Work's good, keeps me busy."

"Still like boys?"

Jimmy laughed, resting a hand on Ralphie's shoulder. "Men, Ralphie, I like men."

"Then get your paw off me."

It was a familiar routine and had both friends grinning. Jimmy watched as a tugboat pushed a large cargo ship out of the harbor, setting it on its course across the Atlantic. The water looked smooth, like glass.

"So, you want to jog my brain again?"

"Before it gets too addled," Jimmy said.

"Might be too late for that."

"Tell me about that day, again."

"Jimmy, you were there. I wasn't."

True, but Ralphie had almost been there, and he knew the details as well as anyone. What Ralphie recounted now was the same as he'd done all these years, and Jimmy concentrated on every word, imagining that one of them could be the missing clue. St. Patrick's Day, a holiday in the McSwain household, Ralphie and Joey were off duty that night after working the parade route, and they finished the night at Paddy's. Drunk as skunks, Joey had insisted Ralphie come back to the apartment, sleep it off. No sense going all the way uptown, which is where he'd lived at the time. So he did, and in the morning Maggie had been less than thrilled to see her husband's partner passed out on the sofa. "Ah, Maggie, you know it's once a year, why do you always got to complain when it's the same damn thing," Joey had said. The way Ralphie told the story, he spoke in Joey's thick neighborhood brogue, with Jimmy allowing a smile of remembrance. Joey had then announced he was going out to grab the newspaper, maybe get some bagels and cream cheese for breakfast. Thick dough, stick to your ribs cheese, good enough to sop up whatever beer and whiskey remained in their systems.

"I'll go," Maggie said, grabbing for her coat.

"Relax. You cooked up a storm last night. Best corned beef of your life, Mags," he said. He kissed Maggie and she rubbed his cheek, telling him he needed a shave and him waving it off like it was a familiar litany. As he opened the door, fourteen-year-old Jimmy came dashing out of his room, sneakers on, coat on. "I'll go too," he said. Joey smiled and said, "That's my boy, helping out your old man when needed. Someday you'll be the man of the house, good way to learn it, watching how it's done."

His voice had almost a wistful tone.

Jimmy knew what came next. The visit to the corner deli, grabbing the *Daily News* and a ordering up a sack of bagels and a carton of pulpy orange juice, everything packed up neat, breakfast at the ready. An argument began in the back of the deli, Joey sneaking a look in the round mirror that enabled the clerk to see the coolers. Joey saw two men, then he saw the glint of metal. So did Jimmy.

"Dad, let's go."

He wasn't Dad now, he was a cop. Taught to respect the law, to keep the calm.

The gun went off even before Joey got to the two men who were fighting, one of the men now on the floor, blood pouring out of him. The other guy ran fast, pushing over a display of Twinkies and Ding Dongs to impede the progress of the man chasing hard after him. That man was of course Joseph McSwain, an off-duty cop assuming command, and it was that man who ran out onto the sidewalk faster than Clark Kent in a revolving door. Jimmy chased after him. The man stopped when Joey called. The assailant turned and, as if the world had slowed, Jimmy watched in horror as the gun spit out its bullet and sliced through the air, hurtling toward its target.

"You know the rest, Jimmy. No need to relive that."

But he did need to, over and over again, often in his dreams, often in his waking hours.

More so now, this time of year.

"Stupid robbery gone bad, your Dad caught in the crossfire."

"So how come the cops never found the guy?"

"Probably they did, Jim, but for something else. Fifteen years later, he's either in jail for another crime or he's dead."

"I think he's out there, still."

"I know you do."

"One day I'll know the truth."

"I know you will."

Jimmy stood up, leaned over the iron rail, and looked at the island of Manhattan, at the wide expanse of the Brooklyn Bridge that connected the boroughs. So many complex lives on these streets, so many stories played out in those buildings, none guaranteed a happy ending. So what assurances did Jimmy have that he'd find his?

He turned away, a rare tear appearing. After all these years, he was so tired of lingering questions, telling himself it was time to seek serious answers. The primary one was who had shot and killed his father, but the second question ranked just as high: Why had the cops dropped the investigation?

"Ralphie, do you think my father knew he was going to die?"

"Why, because of all that stuff about you becoming the man of the house?"

"No, because he knew someone was after him."

"After him? That's nonsense, Jim. Sounds like some crazy conspiracy."

"But what if it wasn't? What if my father knew something?"

"Like what?"

"I'm not so sure," he said, taking a deep breath before he continued, voicing his long-thought suspicions to Ralphie for the first time. "It wasn't a random accident. What happened that day was premeditated murder."

"Jim, don't do this to yourself."

Jimmy just shook his head, almost as though he'd suddenly convinced himself. He thought back to that day, saw the shooter stop and plant himself on the sidewalk right near that fire hydrant, as though he'd already planned it out. "The bullet hit him square in the forehead," he finally said. "My father was executed."

CHAPTER SEVEN

"We're going where?"

"A drag show."

"On a first date?"

"Actually, I think our first date took place in my bed."

Even over a phone line, Jimmy could see a smile. "I like that kind of date."

"Hopefully tonight's ends the same way," Jimmy said. "For now, drag queens await us."

"Guess I should have called you first. Got stuck in a cover meeting, but I meant to text and suggest we have a romantic dinner."

"Sounds nice. But this will be more fun." Jimmy gave him the address.

"I'll, uh, meet you there."

That had been the conversation Friday morning when Jimmy called Barry to confirm their night out. While it had taken a bit of coaxing on his part, the date was set. Now, as nine-thirty rolled around on a crisp March night, Jimmy was in his bedroom, dressed in a pair of jeans and boots, going through his closet for a shirt his mother would approve of. He tried a blue striped one, decided against it and tossed it to the bed. It joined four others in a messy pile. Usually he wouldn't care what he wore, but he was nervous; it had been a while since he'd gone on an actual date.

Not that this was any kind of normal date.

It was part of a case he was working, a detail he'd conveniently kept from Barry.

He felt he'd been giving Harris Rothschild's disappearance short shrift, but at least he'd given Jellison an update, even if he was evasive in revealing what he knew, what he suspected. "I don't have enough to go on, not yet," he'd told her, and no, he hadn't seen him. Jimmy hoped he wouldn't obsess too much on the case tonight, because the last thing he wanted was to ignore Barry.

Jimmy finally settled on a black shirt with a vertical purple pinstripe. The colors looked good on him, he thought, assessing himself in the mirror. Before buttoning, he splashed a dash of Obsession on his chest, rubbed it into his neck. He scratched his chin, wondering if he should have shaved. He hadn't since Tuesday when he met with the Rothschilds, but he figured now he didn't have the time to spare. He left the dark scruff; Barry had liked it. Then he buttoned up his shirt and pronounced himself ready to go. Slipping on his leather jacket, Jimmy departed the apartment just as his mother and sister were walking up the stairs with a couple grocery bags in their hands. His mother was on the early shift tonight, but Meaghan was supposed to have stayed late.

"I switched," she said before Jimmy could even ask.

"None of my business," he said holding up his hands.

"Where are you going looking all studly?" Meaghan asked.

"None of your business."

"Jimmy has a hot date," Maggie said. "He got a call the other night when we were at Paddy's, couldn't so much as talk in front of his mother. Are we to expect you for breakfast?"

"Ma, don't ask those kinds of questions."

"At least she's discreet," Meaghan said. "Come on, who is he? Remy back in town?"

He pointed a finger at her. "Don't. Go. There."

Then he kissed his mother's cheek. "Have a good night, Ma."

He bounded down the four flights, emerging into a starlit night just beginning to pulse. He hailed a cab on Tenth Avenue, told the driver to avoid traffic on Ninth and take Eleventh before swinging over to 22nd Street. In his mind, he was cursing his sister. Leave it to her to bring up the one subject he never wanted to talk about, especially before a date with another guy.

Remy.

Fuck him, he thought, pushing the thought of his ex from his mind.

The picture remained, as did the voice, the French accent.

"I'm sorry, Jimmy, it will never work."

Fortunately the cab got him to Chelsea quickly, where Jimmy found Barry already waiting on the sidewalk in front of the club. He too wore jeans, but he'd worn a sweater, with a long coat and scarf. Stylish. Cute. Had he gotten his hair cut, trimmed his beard? Jimmy saw him, smiled, and then, when he was standing before Barry, he kissed him.

"Hi," he said.

"Hi…ooh, you smell nice."

"Thanks. So, uh, do you like the place?"

The Dress Up Club was all dolled up tonight, pink and blue neon lighting up the street in front of the five-story building. Large posters of the featured performers hung in the windows, each of them surrounded by blinking colored lights. Jimmy stole a look inside, where he saw only a few tables occupied so far. He figured by ten it would fill up.

"I gotta say, Jimmy, I was surprised. I mean, drag queens don't seem your scene."

"What did you expect?"

"I don't know. A baseball game?"

He laughed. "It's spring training, teams are still in Florida."

"Why are they in Florida?"

Jimmy remembered the guy was English, and they knew nothing about American sports. "So cute, accent and all."

He kissed him again, catching the glance of a straight couple entering the club.

"If they've got a problem with two men kissing in Chelsea," Jimmy said, "I don't know what the hell they're expecting inside.

Oh well, they're on our turf. Shall we?"

Jimmy opened the door and allowed Barry to enter first. As they approached the hostess station, Jimmy saw a large figure appear from the back. As she loomed closer, he realized it was Terence Black himself, or perhaps it was appropriate to call the confection before them *her*self. Terry Cloth's makeup was done perfectly, from glittery eyelashes to ruby red lips. Her outfit was hidden, though, of course, beneath a white terry cloth robe.

"Well, if it's not my hunky private eye," Terry said. "So glad you could make it."

"Evening. This is Barry."

"Hello," he said.

"Barry and Jimmy, how darling. Where do I buy the movie?"

"Excuse me?" Barry asked.

"Oh, I'd watch you two do it all night long."

Barry gave Jimmy a worried look. "How do you know…her?"

"I'll explain."

"I saved you a table up front, a private one just for you. You'll find it romantic."

Terry escorted them personally to the table, which provided them with an unobstructed view of the raised stage. Unlike the previous day he was here, the stage now extended into the room like a runway. A baby grand piano was set up against the wall, a microphone stand beside it. A red-sequined curtain covered the back wall, but Jimmy recalled seeing a wall-length mirror there before. The lights were dim but not dark, and he assumed from the disco balls hanging from the ceiling that the club would be awash in color at some point. For now, the two of them could cozy up in their own world.

A waiter approached the table. He wore a red bow tie and tight black pants that left little to the imagination. His chest looked like it had been not only waxed but given a nice polish too, and his abs proved that it wasn't just the bar that had six packs.

"Gentleman, good evening. Terry Cloth tells me you've ordered a bottle of bubbly."

"Uh, no, we didn't…" Barry said.

"I did," Jimmy said. "I called this afternoon."

The waiter took a food order—a tray of light snacks—and moments later he was back with their champagne, the sound of the popping cork catching the attention of the rest of the patrons. Once served, Jimmy raised his flute, watching as the bubbles danced and reflected off Barry's glasses. He toasted, and they drank, but Barry looked hesitant.

"Something wrong?"

"Yeah, this whole night. Jimmy…I don't get it."

He set his glass down and reached out to hold his hand. "I know this is a bit unconventional, I mean, aside from a very nice time the other night, we really don't know much about the other. But trust me, we're here for a reason."

"Care to share that reason?"

Jimmy leaned in so close he could hear Barry's breathing. Then, his voice almost a whisper, he said, "If I told you this was part of a case I'm working, what would you say?"

Barry clasped his hand tightly. "I'd say you just got even sexier, if that's even possible."

"I'll make it up to you another time."

"You can make up for it later tonight."

Jimmy felt excitement flush through his body, settling in his loins.

Their food arrived and the champagne cooled their desires for now. The two of them switched gears, talking about things other than the case—how Barry's first week at the publishing house went, and what he missed already about London. Jimmy told him about his mother, the theatre, anything but what they were really doing here. Because of client confidentiality, he wasn't comfortable telling anyone about his cases, much less a man he'd taken out on a combo date/stakeout. But since he was mixing business and pleasure, he realized he had no choice. He kept things vague.

"I'm looking for a missing person."

"And you think he's here?"

"He, yes," Jimmy said, "or she."

Barry would have to wait for an explanation to Jimmy's enigmatic comment. The show was about to start, and the crowd had burst into applause as entrance music began to play. Musical Mondays at Gaslight had taught him the song was "If You Could See Me Now." Jimmy checked his watch—ten o'clock on the nose—then stared down at the list of performers on the printed program that had been provided. It was the last name that interested him, the drag queen with the following billing: "And Introducing…A Special Guest."

So, there was another first-timer to the Dress Up Club.

Just like him.

§ § §

"Gentlemen, it is my extreme pleasure to welcome you handsome lads to the Dress Up Club. As for you ladies, either you took a wrong turn out of the Lincoln Tunnel, or you're looking for some fashion tips. Otherwise, I don't know what the hell you're doing here."

Laughter spread through the room as Terry Cloth dashed off her *bon mot* with style. The room had filled to capacity, even though the perfume was cheaper than the drinks and the finger food cost at least an arm. Terence Black had a gold mine here. Jimmy had newfound respect for him not only as a businessman, but also as an entertainer. Terry Cloth had finally shed her trademark white robe, letting it drop to the floor to reveal a dress of black sequins that sparkled under the swirling lights. Her cleavage was impressive. False for sure, but nonetheless impressive. She grabbed hold of the microphone and, pointing to Jimmy in the front row, said, "This one's for you, darling."

She then launched into what could only be called a committed performance of the Judy Garland classic "The Man That Got Away," a song he'd seen done recently on Broadway in a show called *End of the Rainbow*. Maggie had had comps and had taken him to the Belasco Theatre. Tonight's crowd applauded appreciatively, and Terry Cloth took an extended bow, curtsying so deep Jimmy could see cleavage. The transformation from nothing to D-size cup was remarkable.

"What are you looking at?" Terry asked with an arched eyebrow, making Jimmy turn red. Turning to Barry, she said, "He likes these. Guess you're outta luck tonight."

Barry looked like he was regretting his decision to cross the pond.

Again, laughter spilled out over the crowd.

"Now, boys…oh, okay, girls, too. No…not you, honey," she said to a razor-thin guy at a corner table. "I meant the real girls, the ones without penises…anyway, ooh, where was I? All this talk of penises gets me all hard, and that shouldn't be happening now, should it? That's what I call a dress up. Now, speaking of dress up, we've got a fabulous with a capital F line-up for you all tonight, and we're gonna start with one of my favorites….Cher and Cher Alike."

"Oh Lord," Barry said, reaching for his glass. "Really?"

They weren't exactly twins, as one of the two Cher impersonators was the 70s version, with long straight hair and a Cherokee Indian outfit. The second was 90s Cher, with crinkly, teased hair and that mesh-like *Flashdance* sweater look. As expected, their routine was filled with off-color jokes and Cher classics, four of them before they got to their finale. That's when Cher and Cher Alike were at their best, with a creepy, but somehow hilarious take on the Sonny & Cher duet "Ie Got You Babe."

The audience was wild for them, but Jimmy sat nearly stone-faced. He felt he'd been assaulted worse just now than when Hickney attacked him. "Sorry," he mouthed to Barry.

They had to endure another act as well, this from a five-foot-six black performer who was as round as he was tall. He wore a yellow dress, again, with daunting-sized breasts underneath it, and so much makeup the Bloomingdale's counter might well want to restock. Terry Cloth, continuing to act as emcee, introduced him as Urethra Franklin.

And yes, she sang "Respect."

Urethra milked the audience participation portion of the song, pointing the microphone toward the crowd to assist her in the spelling. Fortunately, Urethra Franklin's act didn't last as long as the two Chers, and now, as the lights dimmed, a lone spotlight fell on Terry Cloth. A hush fell over the eager crowd. Jimmy felt Barry snake his hand across the table and connect with his. They exchanged smiles through the mist of the spotlight, and Jimmy had to admit this was the nicest stakeout he'd ever been on.

"You owe me big time," Barry said.

Jimmy laughed. "I'm happy for you to call that in any time."

"How about now?"

"I think we've got one more act to sit through, and if my instinct means anything, it's what we've come for."

Just then Terry Cloth reclaimed the stage.

"The moment I've been waiting months for, ladies and gentlemen. I'd like to present our newest convert to the Dress Up Club, a lady of extreme talent and impeccable beauty, a lady who knows just how to strike at your heart...and perhaps at other parts of your body that pulsate. I present to you the one, the only, the delectable...Miss Jellicle Balls."

Jimmy heard the name and nearly spit out his champagne.

He forgot all about Barry for the moment, his eyes focused on the red curtain at the back of the wall. It opened with panache, revealing a slim, perfect figure in silhouette, with curves in all the right places. As the performer stepped forward, Jimmy indeed felt his heart racing. As the pianist began to play, Miss Jellicle Balls clearly meant to dazzle them with her voice. Jimmy saw a stunning woman stepping into the spotlight. He recognized those high cheekbones, the long, silky blonde hair, the richly colored lips not frozen by collagen. She was what his client might once have looked like in her performing days.

Jimmy McSwain had at last come face-to-face with the object of his client's concern, the presumed missing Harris Rothschild.

He was missing all right, even as he stood right before them.

Because Jimmy saw no sign of the man in those photographs.

He wasn't just playing a character, a creation of his mind. This wasn't at all about dressing up. He seemed to inhabit her soul.

And then she opened her mouth, pitch perfect notes streaming out as naturally as clouds drifted through the sky. She wowed everyone from the first note, singing "Memory." When she was done with her lilting, dynamic performance, taking that powerful key change toward the end of the song without trouble, she stretched out her arm and pointed upward at what, in the musical *Cats*, was called the heaviside layer. The audience sat in stunned silence.

And then came the applause, thunderous and earnest.

She'd captured the crowd and now held them in the palm of her hand. And no shills were sitting among them, as Jimmy knew that Miss Jellicle Balls had no family in the audience. She drank in the acclaim, clearly comfortable not just on the stage but in the persona she inhabited. Intrigued, curious, Jimmy stole a look over at Terry Cloth, whose hands were clasped and whose face beamed with pride. He thought he detected a tear rolling down her cheek.

"That's who you came to find?" Barry asked.

Jimmy considered his answer carefully before responding. "She's so convincing I'm surprised she hasn't hired me to find Harris Rothschild too."

CHAPTER EIGHT

The entertainment was at last over, with some members of the audience having paid their bills and departed for whatever else awaited them on a Friday night, while others lingered over a fresh round of drinks, their conversation animated over what they had just seen. Jimmy and Barry did neither. They sat at their table among empty glasses. Jimmy scanned the room, wondering where the lush and lovely Miss Jellicle Balls had gotten off to. Cher and Cher Alike were sitting at the bar, still in full costume, and Urethra Franklin was flitting about—as much as her size allowed—from table to table, chatting up her newfound fans. But Miss Jellicle Balls was nowhere to be found, playing the role of a diva by ignoring those who had made her a star. Either that, or she had retreated back into the shell of her other self, the rather staid, Upper East Side blond and bred Harris Rothschild.

"I don't know about you, Jimmy, but I sort of feel violated after what we saw."

"It was certainly…different. Probably should have taken you to a ballgame."

Barry smiled, his eyes bright behind his lenses. "I guess I just don't get the whole drag culture."

"Don't have that in England?"

"Oh, sure, we have our share of Lady Dianas and Queen Elizabeths, J.K. Rowling…"

"You mean the Harry Potter lady?"

"Hairy Potter? You could play that role."

Jimmy grimaced at the lame joke. "I'll pass."

Barry laughed.. "I'd rather just hang at my local pub. If I'm feeling adventurous, I can always hit the bars on Old Compton Street in Soho. Though come to think of it, there's a pub that does drag, right around the corner on Charing Cross—shit, it's got a funny name…what pub doesn't…oh, the Molly Mogg's.

I've been dragged there a few times."

"Dragged? Really, Barry?"

"Sorry. Unintentional."

"So, tell me more about London, about you."

"Nothing much to tell about me. I live for books, I'm reading all the time for both work and for pleasure and have tons of books back home. I think I miss my bookshelves the most. But don't get me wrong, I do take my nose out of books sometimes. I do like to have fun. Mostly when I go into the West End, I hit Compton's, which is where the young British guys dance and cruise and smile at you. For something less in your face, there's the Admiral Duncan just across the road. The older gays kind of sit there and stare across the street, like looking at lost dreams."

"Poetic. And kind of sad."

"Live it or lose it," Barry said.

"Good philosophy. You know, Barry, I've never been to your…what do they say…side of the pond?" Jimmy said plainly. "Never been much of anywhere, truth be told. Crossing the river to Jersey may as well be crossing a time zone. Guess that makes me a homebody."

"Nothing wrong with that. I like both your home and your body," Barry replied with a suggestive wink. "The only thing we do differently in London is drive on the other side of the road. Otherwise, we like the same positions as you do."

Jimmy's eyes widened at Barry's overtly sexual remark, turning him on in the process and making him think he'd worked the case enough tonight. Barry deserved his attention after the night he'd put him through. But as he was about to suggest they take this back home, Terry Cloth emerged from out of the back room, catching Jimmy's attention. It was the opportunity he needed.

Perhaps he was about to get an audience with the star.

"Hold that thought," he told Barry as he got up from his chair. "I'll be right back.

Terry was once again wrapped up in her white robe, striding

behind the bar to confer with one of those hunky shirtless waiters. Out of the corner of a wary eye, she must have seen Jimmy approach.

"Well, if isn't my favorite private dick," she said.

"Funny. Never heard that before."

She pursed her crimson lips with more than a hint of dissatisfaction. "Someone's in a foul mood? Date not going well?"

"Just fine. We enjoyed the show."

"I'm so glad."

"I'd like to talk to one of your performers."

"Oh," she said, with an arched eyebrow, "and who would that be?"

"Do we really have to dance like this?"

"I'd love to dance with you, honey, feel those muscular arms wrapped around me."

"Just a figure of speech," he said.

"Mine wasn't," Terry said, "but I suppose you already have a man for the night."

"And I could get to spend some alone time with him if you first let me talk to Harris."

"Harris? No one here by that name."

Jimmy knew he was being toyed with, but he didn't let it change his approach or his tone. "I think you've got a true star in the making in with your Miss Jellicle Balls. She was great. The rest...kinda campy."

"May I quote you? I'll have a placard made up tomorrow and post it out front."

"Do that. In the meantime, Harris? Where is he?"

Rather than answer him, Terry went behind the bar, where she popped the cork on a fresh bottle of champagne, pouring out not one, not two, but four glasses. She handed him two of the glasses. "Promise me you'll be nice. There's a fine line between triumph and vulnerability."

"Cross my heart."

"First dressing room to the left. I'll keep your date occupied while you're…busy. Don't blame me if Mr. Cutie From Across the Pond falls head over heels in love with me. I can be quite captivating."

Jimmy nodded. "I'll take that chance."

"Yes, considering he's with you, I do suppose your date goes for the more, shall we say… masculine type. But surprisingly, so does the object of your attention, so if I were you…" she said, pausing she popped open an extra button on his shirt with one of her painted fingernails. "Hmm, very nice indeed. I suggest you try a subtle, seductive approach."

"This is subtle?"

Terry Cloth looked nearly forlorn. "Just don't go in guns blazing. You just might scare the poor, delicate creature."

"I'll be the proper gentleman my mother raised me to be," Jimmy said.

As Jimmy started toward the backstage area, Terry Cloth pulled him back by grabbing hard at his arm. The champagne nearly spilled over his hands. His voice had grown deeper, tinged with a tough of regret.

"I'm serious, don't hurt him, Jimmy. Tonight was a big step in his evolution."

Evolution was a curious word, perhaps a telling one. "Like I said…proper gentleman."

"I'm like a mother hen when it comes to my girls. Hurt them, I'll hurt you."

"I'll be careful."

"And I'll keep your date occupied. Don't be long."

Jimmy considered the idea that Terry Cloth was running more than a drag club here, though what else he couldn't say. It wasn't a sex club. The way he seemed to care for those in his employ, he went beyond the mother hen description. More like a den mother, not just harping but protecting. Terry's female persona was one of sharp barbs and suggestive, pointed remarks, but his male side was tough and aggressive, like a pit bull out to protect its young. Jimmy reminded himself to uncover more about the enigmatic Terence Black, but that would have to wait for another time. For now, the bubbles danced in the glasses he held, and a date with a stranger was just behind the sequined curtain.

He wasn't doing this so much for Saul and Jellison Rothschild. Jimmy was curious not only what made Harris run, but what made him tick. He approached a closed door with a gold star painted in its center. He knocked, careful not to spill the contents of the glasses. He waited.

No reply.

He knocked again, his hand reaching for the knob. It didn't turn.

"Harris...uh, Miss Jellicle Balls, are you in there?"

He thought he detected a sound, perhaps the scrape of a chair. Or it could have been the sound of crying, a heartfelt sniffle. Was he suffering from a post-show letdown or coming to terms with the man he was now—one in women's clothes, a persona that fit him as well as Terry Cloth wrapped herself in Terence Black. Jimmy couldn't pretend to understand what lived inside others. Everyone had their demons; he certainly had his. He thought of his father, he thought too of Harris's father. Funny, one of them would have traded the world to have their father back, the other couldn't distance himself more.

"I don't want to intrude, I..."

The door opened on a combination of two personas. The wig had been removed, but the thick makeup remained, highlighted by a dark streak of mascara down his painted cheek. Jimmy had been right about the tears. Didn't make him feel better. Harris also still wore the dress, but he'd lost his cleavage. The willowy material looked as deflated as the expression in his eyes.

"Knocking loudly on a closed door, bothering someone who craves some alone time," Harris Rothschild said, his choice of words as defiant as his arms-across-his-chest stance. "If that's not the very definition of intrusion, then the privileged education my parents bought has gone to serious waste."

At least he was talking. "Thanks for opening up."

"The door, that's all."

Harris wasn't giving anything up. "No prying, just talk."

"So, you're the private investigator."

"Maybe I'm just a fan." He held out a glass of champagne.

Harris reluctantly accepted one, but set it down on the counter. Then he gazed back and gave Jimmy the once-over. "Terry described you. Very well, I might add."

Despite the fact he loomed over Harris by a good four inches, the usually unflappable Jimmy McSwain felt at a distinct disadvantage. Harris Rothschild was unpredictable, a mix of emotion, a hybrid of identities. But he was being paid to do a job, so he sidestepped Harris and entered the dressing room without being asked. Most of the space was taken up by a rack of sequined, shiny clothes, by a small counter filled with makeup products taking up more space. Light bulbs surrounded a mirror. Jimmy found himself looking into said mirror, staring back at Harris, who still stood with the door open. Harris closed the door, Jimmy watching him in the mirror like a scene in reverse.

"I suppose you've already called them," he said.

"Who?" Jimmy wanted to know how much Harris knew. The glass in his hand was in the way, so he put it on the counter with the other. Neither man was in a celebrating mood.

"My parents, who else? Did they find you in the Gay Yellow Pages?"

"Those would be more rainbow-colored if anything."

Harris attempted an amused look, helped by the overdone rouge. "You really gay or just pretending in order to get close to me?"

"You saw me and the guy I was with, holding hands in the front row."

"He could be your...what do they call them, sidekick?"

"That would make me a super hero, not a P.I."

He switched gears. "You never answered the question about my parents."

"Not that it was asked in the form of a question, but no, I haven't."

"Why not?"

Jimmy shrugged. "Guess I was curious. Why the runaway act, why...this?"

"And you think you can barge your way in here, all macho-like, bullying me?"

"No one's bullying, Harris. The macho part just comes naturally."

"I don't get you," he said.

"What's to get?"

"I mean, you're not like many of the gay guys I know."

Jimmy looked around the dressing room, thought about the other performers. "Don't play into stereotypes, Harris."

"So, Mr. McSwain, what do you want from me, then?"

"Simple. Call your parents. They're worried about you."

"More like mother is anxious, father is hoping I don't do anything that embarrasses him."

"Your act an homage to Jellison or poking fun?"

"Did you laugh during my set?"

Point taken. It had been affecting, powerful, anything but funny. "Look, Harris..."

"No, you look, Mr. McSwain. I can't stop you from telling them you found me."

"That's true."

"But look at me—I've just gone on stage and performed, for the first time, in a drag show in front of a bunch of strangers who came for a night's entertainment. No judgments, not among the audience and certainly not among my fellow queens. I think for the first time in my life, I felt like I was living inside my own skin, I was…comfortable. No, it's more than that. Confident, perhaps. I didn't have butterflies floating in my stomach. Once the piano started and the lights hit me and I looked out and saw the expectant crowd…there's no other word for it. I came alive." He paused, wiping away another string of those mascara-streaked tears. "Are you that eager to get paid that you're willing to jeopardize whatever chance I might have at happiness?"

"Just call your parents and tell them you're okay."

"Then you walk away? Hands clean, job well done. Next case, please."

"Yeah, that's how it works. I'm just the hired muscle," he said. "You do your job, I'll do mine."

"Fuck you."

"Tough words coming from such a lady," Jimmy said.

The remark actually eased the tension that had been building inside the room.

Jimmy started toward the door, realizing he wasn't going to get anywhere.

"Give me twenty-four hours," Harris said.

Jimmy turned back around. "Here's my card. Call me when you're ready to talk to them. I can help facilitate."

Harris swallowed, his Adam's apple visible beneath the coating of base.

Again, Jimmy observed that the beautiful Harris Rothschild wasn't quite sure of his own identity. Perhaps he wondered which of them he would reveal to his parents. Miserable male, or fabulous female. Did dressing up in women's clothes satisfy whatever he lacked inside him, or did the pathology go deeper? Time enough for those questions another day. He'd accomplished what he set out to do tonight. He'd found his client's son.

He opened the door and stepped out.

He thought he could hear weeping coming from inside the dressing room.

§ § §

Heat occupied another room, far from the dressing room of the Dress Up Club.

By the time Jimmy and Barry arrived at the second-floor office on Ninth Avenue, the anticipation between them boiled, threatening to explode. When they entered the apartment and closed the door, their mouths connected with fiery passion, their hands exploring with intensity. Barry cupped Jimmy's ass and pulled him in tight. Jimmy grabbed at Barry's crotch, feeling him thicken. He watched as Barry undid the remaining buttons of his shirt and peeled the shirt off his shoulders. Barry immersed himself in the thick hair of his chest, seeking out buried nipples with his tongue. Jimmy closed his eyes and allowed every delicious kiss.

They fell to the sofa, not bothering to open it. Passion first, comfort later.

Clothes removed the two men came at each other with fierce drive.

Soon Barry was on his back, legs in the air. He opened up and Jimmy went at him fast, went at him hard, with relentless fire, the rocking motion making the springs squeak. Jimmy thrust his hips with demanding passion.

"Oh Jimmy...Jimmy...do me, yeah...oh, yeah, fuck me hard."

Their attraction had only grown since their first night together. Then it had been all about the physical and now, tonight, this moment, as their shadows danced an erotic dream upon the walls, a deeper connection established itself. Maybe it was because of the lonely souls they had seen tonight, those faraway looks in their eyes despite dedication to their performances, dressing up to forget whom they were, that both men were eager to express what existed inside them. Honesty, truth, swirling emotions and feelings brought to urgent, physical life by their steamy coupling.

Jimmy continued fucking Barry, feeling the man's fingers dig into the meat of his back. He held him tight, he held him close, urged him on. Jimmy pounded him, sweat dripping down his face and catching in the hollow of his throat. A few drops embedded themselves in his chest hair and Barry sucked them up, tasting him. Asking for more.

"Harder, oh man, don't stop…more…"

But more eventually gave way to a final moment of intensity. Barry grabbed at his chest hair, and the sensation rocked him until his cock thickened and opened up. He felt the rush through the shaft, and finally come burst from the tip. He felt ropes shoot out, each one forcing his hips into another wild thrust. Barry too climaxed at that point, his come pooling on his chest, mingling with Jimmy's as he collapsed atop him while he sought breath.

They lay entwined, silenced and satisfied, and it was only after Jimmy had fetched two beers that they finally spoke, their words no longer flavored with the heat of their intense love-making. The pounding of flesh upon flesh was replaced by a newfound, satisfied silence, a gentle caress.

"What just happened?" Barry asked.

"I think the drag queens reminded us that we are men."

"You came at me so hard, so fast."

Jimmy took a pull on his beer. "Not too fast, I hope."

"That's not what I meant…"

"Besides, you practically had my clothes off in the cab."

"Your shirt was already half-open when we left the club."

"Terry Cloth's fault. She may be the mother hen, but I think she prefers Daddies."

Barry slid a hand across Jimmy's pelt. "I love how this feels, especially when you're inside me."

Jimmy kissed him, felt Barry tighten his grip on a thick tuft. "So, we didn't have a chance to talk much, not our first night, not tonight."

"So this is when we get to know each other beyond the biblical sense?"

"Was what we did in the Bible?"

"Jimmy McSwain, I think your good Catholic mother would strike you down."

"I'd rather God did it. Maggie McSwain's wrath is probably worse."

"You're awful," he said. "In a good way."

"Just good?"

Barry laughed. "I came back for more, didn't I?"

"Tell me about you, your job," Jimmy asked. "I should know more about you."

"Pillow talk, Jimmy?"

"Words help. It can't just be physical."

"I like the physical."

"You're avoiding the topic."

Leaning to his side, brushing Jimmy's chest lazily, Barry opened up. "Like I said, it's a three-month exchange program with our U.S. parent. I'm an editor, so I'm supposed to get to know more literary agents in New York. The same is true for my counterpart. She's to get to know the agents and publishers in London. Publishing is increasingly a world community, even more so today when so much of the industry is in flux."

"Can't tell you the last time I read a book," Jimmy said.

"Good, so I don't have to bore you with the details of my job."

"Back at ya," Jimmy said.

"Well, your job is way sexier than mine. To think, I was on a stakeout with you."

"Hardly a typical stakeout. We knew where the perp was."

"Perp. Ooh, I like when you use your P.I. lingo," Barry said.

They kissed again, hungrily, Jimmy's hand snaking downward, finding Barry excited all over again. He stroked him and their eyes connected ; the message exchanged clearly. In a moment, Jimmy climbed over him, Barry's legs open once more. He entered him with greater intensity, Barry crying out with desire. As Jimmy thrust at him repeatedly, hard, he felt Barry's fingers dig into his back, his legs curled around his ass. They were locked, loaded, they were bonded, they were one, and they rode out the building passion with energy, the night forgotten, the pains of others a distant memory. This was now, this was here, and the two of them rode out whatever deeper hurts were lost inside them and hadn't been shared.

"Jimmy...I never had it like this..."

Jimmy pounded him, and soon he felt the climax boil inside him. His body froze with anticipation, and then the heat flushed through him. He cried out as he thrust once more, Barry biting down on his shoulder as he embraced his lover, his release.

At last Jimmy came to a rest, and he fell over onto the blanket.

Barry cradled him. "Tell me something totally hot," he said, stroking himself.

Jimmy laughed. "Like what?"

"Have you ever shot someone?"

Jimmy felt the room darken, as though swallowing him whole.

He saw nothing but a burst of fire, he heard nothing but a familiar, tortured cry.

It was too much to hear in the supposed comfort of the arms of a man who was really nothing more than stranger to him. He'd gone down the wrong path, asked the wrong question. Jimmy wanted him gone now, just like the memories. He got up fast, ignoring Barry's question. Still naked, he felt exposed, like Barry could see through him. Like he'd opened up a hole, only Jimmy couldn't hide inside it.

"Jimmy...I'm sorry...what did I say?"

Jimmy didn't want to answer him. Luckily his cell phone rang. The shrill sound felt louder than it was in the quiet of the night. He looked at the clock and was surprised to see it was almost dawn. They'd been fucking all night.

Still, calls at five in the morning were never a good sign. Almost like Barry's question was an omen.

He didn't recognize the number, but he always picked up. Danger was anonymous.

"This is Jimmy."

"This...this is Harris Rothschild," came a trembling, tenuous voice.

"Harris, is everything okay?"

Stupid question. He knew otherwise. Not even the moon outside seemed to give off light.

"No...not at all."

"What's going on?"

"I...I...don't know what happened. But my father's dead."

PART TWO

A DEVIL AMONG THEM

CHAPTER NINE

Harris's words reverberated in his mind long after the phone call had ended.

"My father's dead."

How often had he spoken that very same phrase, his heart frozen in fear? Countless times, endless times, at all times during the day, and now as a new dawn rose. But despite his feelings, this wasn't about him. This was part of the job. He had to see Harris.

One of the only advantages of trekking outside at five in the morning was the availability of cabs. Barry took the first one to stop on the corner of Ninth Avenue and 45th, having parted with a bittersweet kiss that felt like a final one to Jimmy. He had a feeling he'd freaked Barry out with his reaction to the question of whether he'd ever shot someone. It had reopened a wound barely healed. Jimmy wasn't proud of how he'd handled things, but this was not a time of day for life decisions. Darkness enjoyed too much its mysteries and hidden motives. Underneath the near-black sky that had yet to give up all its dead, Jimmy was journeying back downtown to the Dress Up Club, where he found Terence at the front door, awaiting his arrival as soon as the cab let him out.

A scrape of light made its way across the sky, the first indication a new day loomed. For some.

"Where's Harris?"

"Upstairs."

"And Saul…his father?"

He shook his head. "For that you'll have to ask the police."

Police. Of course they were involved. But at least Harris wasn't in custody. Jimmy knew so few of the details, yet he was convinced the son had killed the father. What else would make sense?

Supposition was one thing, facts another. It was the latter Jimmy sought.

"Want to tell me what happened?"

"Come in, Jimmy," Terence said, ushering him inside the club.

Jimmy followed Terence past the dressing rooms and through a pass door, which led to a back staircase. They went solemnly to the second floor and entered one of the front apartments. Jimmy had scoped out four doors, two in the rear, two in the front, a typical Manhattan walk-up. Harris paced the carpeted floor, fully divested of any trace of his Miss Jellicle Balls persona. It was Jimmy's first look at his natural state, and he still thought the young man could only be described as beautiful.

"Thank you for coming so quickly," he said, turning from the window where he'd let go of the curtain.

Jimmy surmised this was the so-called woman who had stared back at him the other day from the upstairs window. Had Harris known then that Jimmy had been looking for him? The apartment was sparse, the furniture not the best quality but serviceable and comfortable. Otherwise, few personal items adorned the walls and shelves, giving the apartment a sense of transience. As if Harris could disappear into the ether in seconds, leaving behind barely a fingerprint.

"I'm glad you called," Jimmy said. "Your words…"

"I didn't mean to shock you. Probably woke you."

"Don't worry about it. Unconventional hours come with the job."

"Still, you didn't have to come."

"Your father was my client."

"My father obviously didn't trust you."

Jimmy had thought as much already in the cab ride down. He supposed Saul Rothschild had set a tail on his own private investigator, perhaps even from his initial hiring. Jimmy tried to think back. Had he noticed someone following him and Jellison around the Central Park reservoir? At lunch the other day with

Sissy Hinckley, had someone paid too much attention to what they were discussing? Damn shame he hadn't anticipated such a scenario. But it was all water under the bridge, or perhaps blood, and what mattered most was what had happened.

"He showed up at the club, I don't know…five minutes after closing."

"I had just doused the outside lights and sent the final patrons out into the night," Terence said. "Then there came a loud knock at the door. I tried to send whoever it was away, telling him we were closed for the night, but he wouldn't take no for an answer. Also, he wasn't my typical late-night customer, not with his fancy threads. He had this airy, rich quality to him, someone used to getting their way, entitled. Before I knew what to do, his voice grew angry and he nearly broke the glass door with his fist. While I came around the bar, that's when Harris emerged from the dressing room. And I realized who our guest was."

"I'd just done a last minute set for the club's die-hards," Harris said.

"No wonder you had trouble getting rid of folks," Jimmy said. "You're good."

"Well, not everyone would agree with you."

"I'm guessing the one who disapproved won't be around to disapprove a second time."

"He watched me perform through the window. From the sidewalk."

"My walls are sound-proofed," Terence explained. "But pedestrians can still get a sneak peek. Sometimes we get the curious to come in right off the street."

Jimmy looked at Harris, who was staring down at the floor. He wondered if that was significant. Perhaps this was where he and his father went, where an argument ensued. He scanned the floor for blood marks, but didn't see any. Besides, wouldn't a chalk outline have indicated the body had been found here? What had the chain of events been?

"I tried to get away from him. The last thing I needed tonight was confrontation."

"Harris had just triumphed," Terence said. "He should have been able to enjoy the high."

"My father followed me upstairs. We argued."

"Over your performance? Your having disappeared?"

"Over everything," Harris said. "He threatened to cut me off from my inheritance, but I reminded him I didn't care about the money, that I'd walked away from his controlling ways. Funny thing. He's gone, but his will remains unchanged, and I'll inherit despite the cruel words he lashed at me. Not that I want it, but it can do such good for others…God, I don't even know why I'm talking about this. He's barely cold." He paused, a shock wave hitting him, as though reality was settling in. He looked up at a crack in the ceiling before zeroing back in on them. "I hated my father. I hated all that he stood for, and I hated his manipulations of others. Treating me and my mother like hostile witnesses in his courtroom. But I loved him, too. He made sure we never lacked for anything. I suppose it was his way of protecting me. Does that make sense?"

"Parental relationships can be complicated," Terence said quietly, apparently speaking from experience.

Jimmy said nothing..

"Finally, my father stormed out, but not before…"

Harris paused, his lips trembling.

"Harris, you don't have to go there…."

"No, admitting what he did, what he said, I have to face it," Harris said. "He came at me. He smacked me right across the face. The mark has only now just faded. Then he called me…"

Jimmy nodded. He didn't need to hear it. He knew.

But Harris had to say it, to try and move on. "A fucking girl, a faggot."

Jimmy felt a tight knot hit his throat, had trouble swallowing its weight down. People were fucking idiots, passing judgment over others like they were better. If Saul Rothschild had been here now, Jimmy might have smacked him back. But he had to control the situation, try and get Harris to see both sides. "He didn't understand you, Harris, not the real you. His brain didn't know how to process…you," Jimmy finally said, unsure why he was defending Rothschild. Not all fathers who disappeared from their son's lives need be remembered, much less revered or even forgiven.

"As I reeled from his physical and verbal assault, he left."

"How'd he die?"

Harris wasn't ready to jump to the end of the story, the end of his father's life. More details were forthcoming. "I watched from this window as he made his way across the street. I thought it was odd, he'd left the limo and driver home and come out alone, or maybe it was around the corner…I just don't know. All of a sudden I heard a pop…"

"A bang," Terence added.

"A loud one that crackled in the night. There was no sound of struggle, no cry of surprise."

Just bang, shot, dropped, gone. Jimmy knew the feeling. He could see the scene.

"Did you see the assailant?"

Terence shook his head. "It was dark. The shooter never emerged from his hiding spot."

Jimmy nodded. Lying in wait. Saul Rothschild had been followed, targeted.

"I'm sorry, Harris," Jimmy said.

By now Harris had retreated to the far corner of the room. Jimmy saw him slip a blonde wig over his head, as if trying to immerse himself in another person. Terence went over to him, cradled him in a tight embrace, and soon the room's silence was taken up by the sound of wracking sobs that brought Harris Rothschild to his knees.

Jimmy watched the scene unfold.

A shattered Harris, a supportive Terence.

What was the relationship between these two and, for that matter, the other men who performed at the club? Jimmy was beginning to get a sense the Dress Up Club was more than just entertainment. He recalled Terry Cloth's mother hen remark. This place, not only the club but the apartment building, was a refuge. A sanctuary designed to save lives.

Except for tonight.

§ § §

So much for discretion in this case.

His demanding client was no longer around to complain, but that didn't stop Jimmy from hearing him screaming about the press's fixation on the shocking murder. The rich, influential, and powerful Saul Rothschild being gunned down in Chelsea in the middle of the night in front of club known for drag queens was front page news for both the *Post* and the *Daily News*.

DRAGGED TO DEATH, said the former.

NO MAKEUP DATE, said the latter.

Humorless, sensationalistic, one of the papers even went so far as to airbrush lipstick on Saul's otherwise aristocratic face to help sell the early edition. Such was the world of the New York tabloids. Jimmy had seen more clever headlines, no doubt he'd live to see worse. He had grabbed both at the local deli after leaving his mother's apartment, where he'd stopped at seven in the morning to grab two hours of sleep, shower, and change. As he hit the stoop and the day's fresh sunshine hit his eyes, he saw his sister Mallory approaching from the corner. He reached for his sunglasses and slipped them on.

"Not so fast," she said.

"I'm kind of in a rush," he said.

"Your client is in the morgue. I think you've got a minute."

He pulled off the glasses. This moment called for an honest

exchange. "Mallory, you're not blaming me…"

"I recommended you for the job," she said indignantly.

"Yeah, and no matter who Rothschild hired, it wouldn't have mattered. Looks like he didn't trust me to do the job, so he took matters into his own hands. He's dead," he said, his tone angry. "So don't shoot the messenger…or the private eye."

"Not funny," she said.

He had to agree. He wished sometimes he thought before he spoke.

"Sorry," he said.

"No, I am. I'm just…" She couldn't find the word.

Jimmy doubted it existed.

Mallory crossed her arms, lawyer-defiant. "Saul…he just wanted to find his son."

"Yup. And I was his pawn. He paid me good money to find Harris, then he took over."

"Isn't that how it's supposed to go? You work for who pays you."

"It's not that cut-and-dry. It had to be handled delicately. It wasn't."

"Jim, this is my job…my livelihood."

"What, you think you're gonna get fired because one of the firm's top senior partners was murdered?"

"Manhattan law firms are feeding frenzies of gossip and backstabbing."

"And you're one of their top sharks. You'll be fine."

"I better be."

"Tell you what. You get fired, you can come work for me."

"What do you pay with, food stamps?"

Standing on the stoop as the morning sun beamed down on them, brother and sister simultaneously glared and smirked at each other. Jimmy kissed her on the cheek and said he had to run off to an appointment.

"On a Saturday?"

"You think a private eye keeps banker's hours?"

"Are you going to the Rothschilds?"

"Yes," he said, not wanting to lie. "And no, you're not coming with me."

As he started off the last of the steps, she grabbed at his sleeve, worry written on her face. "Jimmy, be careful. I thought it was a simple case."

"Should have been, but Rothschild upped the stakes without informing the dealer."

"Watch your back."

"I've made it this far," Jimmy replied, then bounded off the cement steps, picking up his pace like the New Yorker he was, bypassing elderly ladies with carts out for their morning grocery shopping, past kids on scooters headed to the park with weary fathers trying to keep up. Normal Saturday for most, but not for Jimmy.

He arrived at the 50th Street subway station at Eighth Avenue, went down the stairs on the Uptown/Queens side, and sliced his way through the turnstile courtesy of his Metrocard before hopping down another flight of stairs to await the E train. It rumbled in five minutes later, and he rode it three stops to 53rd and Lex, where he walked that horribly long transfer to the 6 train, rode four more stops and got off at 77th Street. Sounded complicated, but it was like second nature, the subway system the best way to get around. He busied himself on his trip with the headlines. In just a few more minutes, he was back topside and found his way to the Rothschild's imposing building. He discovered two vans parked nearby, satellite dishes positioned on their roofs, one of them from the local Fox affiliate, the other ABC-7. Hell, where were the others? Not like anything else of note had happened last night in Manhattan.

He didn't want to approach the front entrance. He didn't want to attract attention.

Sure, now Jimmy was being discreet.

Jimmy withdrew his cell phone, dialed Jellison, and waited as it rang. It went to voicemail, where he left a quick message to call him back. While he waited, he crossed Fifth and bought a pretzel from the busy vendor just outside the Met. The salt fueled his tired body after a long night of sex, murder, and not sleeping. He asked for a bottle of water and downed it in one gulp, only to find his phone ringing.

"This is Jimmy."

"I assume you're nearby."

"Across the street."

"Service entrance."

"So I thought. I should pass, I'm blue collar enough."

"Bring a wrench to make sure."

"I think your husband tossed that into the works already."

Steering clear of nosy reporters who would love to know that Rothschild hired a P.I. days before his murder, Jimmy went around the corner, buzzed a side entrance to the building and was let in immediately. A doorman came around and pointed him toward the service elevator. Unlike the one he rode the other day, this one didn't let him off inside the apartment. So he went down the hall, prepared to knock. The door opened when he was still ten feet away.

"That elevator makes a lot of noise. I've complained."

"I see they've listened well."

Jellison Rothschild, her eyes puffy, her face devoid of makeup, didn't appear to be in the mood for his smart remarks. Jimmy instructed himself to shut up as he entered the apartment. He felt trapped inside and wasn't sure just what he was in for. A widow intent on hurling blame? A vulnerable soul who'd lost her husband? But Jellison had been a performer even before she was a mother or a wife, so she wiped away tears in dramatic fashion, patting her blonde helmet. In her movements, he saw Harris, or perhaps what he recognized was Miss Jellicle Balls. Her mannerisms were more than impersonation.

Jellison wasted little time. "Have you seen Harris?"

"Twice," he said.

"Twice?"

"Before and after. I didn't tell you or Saul that I'd found him because Harris asked me to give him twenty-four hours to sort out what he wanted to do. I put his feelings above the job."

Jellison seemed to understand. "I woke up in the middle of the night, and Saul was gone."

"He'd gone on a fishing expedition," Jimmy said. "I was the bait."

"I'm sorry, Jimmy."

"So you knew he was having me followed?"

"Saul trusted no one," she said coldly. "He'd already hired someone to follow you when you came to lunch. He figured the easiest way to find his gay son was to hire a gay private eye. Saul found strange comfort in his close-mindedness."

Jimmy noticed she was already using the past tense to refer to her husband. "Did his lack of trust include you?"

"He figured I'd have a soft spot for you."

"Transference."

"You a private eye or psychiatrist?"

"My uncle's a bartender, but slinging drinks is only part of the job."

She nodded wanly. Then she switched topics, the society hostess she had become taking over. "I'd offer you coffee, but I haven't had the energy to make it."

"Why don't you let me do that? Have a seat, I'll be back."

"No, I'd rather have the company. This way," she said, leading him past the living room and the dining room, to a kitchen that was the size of Jimmy's entire office. He thought of the hotplate he kept, boiling coffee until it tasted like tar. It might have been bad, but it usually woke him up. Jellison pointed him toward the far counter.

"Make it easy on us," she said, pointing to a Keurig machine.

He made a Green Mountain hazelnut for himself and a Sleepytime tea for her, thinking she could use some rest. Soon they were settled on wooden stools with soft, floral-printed cushions. He sipped at his coffee, grateful for not just the fragrant smell but the impact. It had been a long night, and the short rest he'd gotten earlier hadn't done the trick. This caffeine infusion helped.

"Thank you, Jimmy," she said with a sense of relief.

"Coffee? Easy."

"That's not what I mean."

He nodded and drank. "If I haven't said it yet, I'm sorry. About Saul."

She stared blank-faced, not ready for condolences. "Do you know anything?"

"It's only been a few hours," he said. "Harris phoned me."

"The papers didn't have all the details, and the police detectives didn't offer much."

"They've been here already?"

"A brief meeting. They said they'd be back. Often."

Jimmy nodded, wondering who'd been assigned the case. That could wait. For now this woman needed comfort, and Jimmy wished her son was the one offering it.

"Harris is fine," Jimmy said. "Physically."

"I appreciate that," she said before switching gears. "Jimmy, I know you have no reason to trust me, not after Saul's deception."

"That's him, you're you."

"Is everything always so black and white with you?"

"Until someone colors my judgment, yeah."

She paused a moment, looking at Jimmy thoughtfully. "I want to hire you," she said.

Jimmy set his coffee cup down. "To do what?"

"Find my husband's killer."

"Isn't that a job for the police?"

She looked at him with surprise. He supposed he sounded naive.

Jimmy had begun this morning thinking he was out of a job, the remainder of his retainer to be returned. Now he was employed again, and the stakes had been upped.

He'd found his missing person.

Could he find a killer?

He thought of his own father, dead almost fifteen years. His killer still free, the case cold.

Could he bring closure for one family when he couldn't for his own?

"I'll get started right away."

CHAPTER TEN

He hated when his cases merged with an active police investigation.

It was one thing for Jimmy to handle his own clients, trail a wayward husband or wife, dig into a person's questionable background, expose a fraud or a lying cheat. Those were his bread and butter and kept him going on the mean streets. When a case comes smeared with actual blood, things take a decidedly darker turn. A life was lost, a family shattered, unfulfilled dreams obliterated with the single blast of a gun, isn't that what the press always seemed to focus on? The victim as saint, the assailant not fit for society. Jimmy always wondered how the criminal felt while watching news of a manhunt for him. How had his deadly action, whether impulsive or premeditated, altered him? Did it make him that much more dangerous, a career criminal realizing he had nothing left to lose, so why not go out in a blaze of glory while on the prowl for his next victim. Or was he burrowed deep somewhere, a wounded animal, cornered, shocked by what he had done and uncertain of his next move. One scenario painted danger, the other desperation.

Reading the mind of a killer sometimes took knowing the moves of the victim.

Since leaving the Rothschild duplex, Jimmy had pondered one thing: Had Saul's murder been random, a rich man out at a time he shouldn't be, falling victim to wrong place/wrong time, or had he been specifically targeted, perhaps by a disgruntled client? It had probably been years since the senior partner at the law firm of Acton, Rothschild, Sutter & Hartley had seen serious courtroom action, much less associated with the criminal element. Saul Rothschild was the type to keep his hands clean, at least in the eyes of his associates, having gone all corporate spreadsheets and high-powered lunches, all while doling out cases to the lesser tenured members of his firm. Among them, his sister, Mallory.

But it wasn't yet time to deal with lawyers. The cops had the case first.

So Jimmy set out for the 10th Precinct on that late Saturday afternoon.

The weather couldn't make up its mind if mid-March was winter or spring. Out of the sunshine, a persistent chill permeated the air, only to disappear as Jimmy crossed the street and felt the sun's warm rays hit his face. He'd stick to the glare. He'd felt enough of a cold front already today. Death had a way of doing that, especially this time of year. St. Patrick's Day was less than a week away, which meant so too was what he thought of as St. Joseph's Day. When his father went violently to his grave.

Jimmy had mixed feelings about cops.

He probably would have been one had that fateful day not occurred.

But it had, and here he was, working on their side of the law but on his own terms.

He reached West 20th Street and the corner of Eighth Avenue, turned down the block to a sea of blue-and-white NYPD cruisers parked at angles on the street. It was easier for them to pull out during an emergency that way, none of that parallel parking nonsense. A couple of officers leaned against their cars, talking on phones or drinking coffee. One of them nodded Jimmy's way. He nodded back as he grabbed the door of the precinct. He could socialize later. First he wanted to know who, besides himself, had the case.

"Well, look what the cat dragged in," someone said.

Jimmy looked around. "You got strays in this neighborhood?"

"Just the one I'm looking at."

From her lofty perch above the high desk, dispatch officer Wren Parker flashed a pearly white smile his way. She was fresh-faced and young, not more than thirty. Over the years of their association, she'd decided she liked giving him a hard time. Jimmy preferred to think it was because she had a major crush but couldn't have him. Wren always told him it was because he was a pain in the ass.

The precinct was slow this sunny day, almost like the crooks had taken a day off to let New Yorkers enjoy their first taste of spring. Phones rang, and the office bustled, but it was the normal course of action, the daily life on the blue line.

"How goes it, Wren?"

"Fine. What, nothing doing Midtown North?"

"Might be, I don't know. I'm here."

"Which means you want something."

"Can't a guy come and say hello?"

"Guys in this neighborhood don't say hello to girls."

Touche, Jimmy thought. This was Chelsea, home to an abundance of gay men who had helped gentrify and re-energize what had once been a seedy neighborhood. As such, it was one of the last places a cute, young thing like Wren Parker would find a date.

"Captain around?"

"Who are you looking for?"

"O'Connell."

She shook her head. "Transferred, Bronx 42nd."

"Tough place. No one better for it. Who you got now?"

"Young stud from Brooklyn, all of thirty-five," she said, her tone less than thrilled. "Fast Track Kid, they call him. Accent and all."

"He got a name?"

"Frisano."

"Sounds connected," Jimmy said.

"I wouldn't advise you start with that," she said. "So, what's got your interest?"

"Last night's murder," he said. "Rothschild."

"Oh, the rich, married lawyer. Sniffing for something he shouldn't be?"

Jimmy shook his head. "He was a client of mine."

That raised an eyebrow. "You come to ask questions or give answers?"

"Probably both."

"It's Roscoe's case. He and Dean. They're not here."

He knew them both, one professionally and the other from the neighborhood. Roscoe Barone was the lead detective, and he didn't spend much time in the office. He was old school. Liked to work on his own time and his own schedule. Larry Dean was a local kid, a couple years ahead of Jimmy at P.S. 111, and he was known as a by-the-book cop who held no power. He was stuck playing by whatever rules his partner lived by. Lately, it was Roscoe.

"But you know where they are."

"Could be anywhere. You know how it goes, first twenty-four are the most important."

"Don't bullshit me with cadet-speak. Where are they?"

"Westside Tavern."

"NYPD paying rent on that place?"

Wren had no response, and Jimmy thanked her for the info and headed back outside.

The Westside Tavern was a short walk along a bustling 23rd Street, and as he came upon its façade, he saw the Moonstruck Diner, where just days ago he'd met with Sissy Hickney. He hoped she was doing okay, then he wondered about the inner struggles Richard Hickney must be awash in. Not his problem. Sissy had paid him, and he'd done as asked, a bit more actually. His thoughts turned to his current case. Harris Rothschild and his mother, Jellison were the ones seeking answers now, and he hoped to find some inside this Chelsea stalwart.

Six people sat along the bar, staring at the television screen like all good barflies. A pool table went ignored in the back, and a stereo system played an old Depeche Mode song. He wasn't sure which one. They all had that suave electronic tone. He noticed Larry Dean sitting on a high stool, a half-empty beer before him. Another empty beer sat at the round table in the corner, but Jimmy didn't see Larry's partner-in-drink.

Larry Dean caught sight of Jimmy.

"Jimmy McSwain, this a coincidence?"

"You believe in them?

"Nope."

"Then, no it's not a coincidence," he replied. "Where's Roscoe?"

Dean looked at the empty glass. "Seeing a man about a horse."

Jimmy had never understood that old phrase, but he let it slide today without explanation. Instead, he backtracked, ordered three Yuenglings from a tattooed bartender and plopped down a twenty, carrying the pint glasses over to the table just as the burly, florid-faced Lieutenant Roscoe Barone exited the men's room. The music changed to Coldplay, "Clocks."

Time indeed was passing, and none of them were getting any younger.

Saul Rothschild wouldn't get any older.

"McSwain," Roscoe said, scorn in his voice.

"Hello, Roscoe."

Cops were funny creatures, suspicious by nature, and doubly so when they were elevated to the position of detective. No one called him Barone, in direct contrast to Dean, who preferred going by his last name. Nothing cool sounding about calling a detective Larry. Like when New York Mets fans chanted "Larry" at Atlanta Brave Chipper Jones, mocking him with his birth name, usually moments before he sent them home in misery with a long ball that cleared the bases. Not unlike those fans, neither detective looked happy to see him, Dean's dour expression following Roscoe's lead. Like always.

The beers, though, were enough of a peace offering to get Jimmy welcomed to the table.

"What brings you here?" Roscoe asked.

"I've got some information for you," Jimmy said. "And I hope you've got some for me."

"You first, then we'll see."

Jimmy took a sip of his beer, and the cops did the same. Not exactly a toast, but it sufficed.

"Saul Rothschild," Jimmy said.

"Aw shit," Roscoe said. "You mixed up in that?"

"You want me to talk or are you going to interrupt each time I open my mouth?"

Roscoe drank, his message clear: talk, I'll listen.

So Jimmy talked, about how he came to know the Rothschilds, why they hired him. The detectives listened, neither taking notes, just sips. As Jimmy told his tale of discovering Harris Rothschild at the Dress Up Club, Roscoe held his expression tight. Old school as he was, alternative lifestyles still hadn't caught up to him, even considering Chelsea was his beat. He'd had his share of cases of guys found murdered in their homes, tied up, gagged, robbed, and the perp turned out to be a trick hired for some kinky sexual shenanigans. What Roscoe did like was the fact that those kinds of sensationalistic cases made the papers and evening newscasts and kept his profile high within the ranks of the NYPD when he solved them. The Rothschild case ranked even higher, making solving it a priority.

Jimmy was finishing as much of the story as he was going to give.

"I left the club around one o'clock," Jimmy said.

"Someone can vouch for that?"

"Is that your way of asking if I was on a date?"

Dean snickered. Roscoe sipped. "Helps to have an alibi."

"Why would I kill my source of income?"

Roscoe shrugged. "So how come the widow Rothschild didn't mention any of this?"

"Guess she wasn't sure it was relevant."

"You talked to her?"

"A few hours ago. She hired me to find Saul's killer."

"Stay out of it, McSwain," Roscoe said. "This is serious stuff. Commissioner Bratton wants results."

"Last I knew, results weren't exclusive to the cops."

"The son never said anything about your involvement either."

Dean intervened. "How'd you hear about the murder, anyway? Wake up with your date? Did you read him the paper in bed?"

Jimmy didn't rise to the bait. Dean wasn't worth it. "Obviously I knew before the press. Harris called me, I guess just after you guys left."

"Fucking early morning call. I hate them," Roscoe said.

"Yeah, you look like you've been losing out on your beauty sleep."

Roscoe finished his beer, looking at Dean as if he should too. He had to chug.

"Thanks for the beer, McSwain. And for coming to us with what you know."

"Well, I was kind of hoping you'd tell me something."

Rising from his seat and putting on his ratty blazer, Roscoe smiled. "You'd think, right?"

"Come on, Roscoe, gimme one thing."

"The perp must have panicked, because he dropped the gun," he said. "We retrieved it. Ballistics says it's stolen, no prints. No identification number."

"Indicates premeditation," Jimmy said.

"Says one theory," Dean answered back.

The two detectives made their way out of the tavern, leaving Jimmy to his thoughts and the last dregs of his brew. Neither left him satisfied.

§ § §

Saturday night, Jimmy found himself in front of the Calloway Theatre, waiting for his mother. The night had turned cold, and flurries were in the forecast. Such were the vagaries of the weather in March, not quite a lion, not quite a lamb. He zipped up his leather jacket, protecting him against the elements as he waited for the show to let out.

"Ten more minutes," said Kitty, the ticket-taker who manned the front lobby.

"Thanks, Kit," he said.

Down the street, the Brooks Atkinson had just opened its doors, and hundreds of people filled the street. The Samuel Friedman, once the heralded, historic Biltmore, was dark right now, and the neighboring Barrymore Theatre had a ninety-minute play, so it was all closed up. This was Broadway on a Saturday night, when throngs of ticket holders went from the closed off streets of Times Square to the tight confines of these landmarked old theatres, some of them in operation since the early nineteen hundreds.

He took advantage of the downtime and pulled out his cell phone, staring at the list of recent calls. Barry's name was third down, after his mother and Jellison Rothschild. He'd called Barry twice, once around noon, after returning from the Upper East Side, again after finishing his meeting with the unhelpful detectives from the 10th. Barry hadn't picked up either time, and Jimmy hadn't left messages. What was he going to say, anyway? Sorry always sounded insincere on voicemail.

So then why had he called? Did he really want him to answer?

Jimmy knew he'd snapped unnecessarily at Barry last night. Rather than explain why, he'd suggested he might want to leave. So why would Jimmy call a third time? No doubt Barry saw the missed calls, and he'd not seen fit to return either. Maybe this time he would pick up, or maybe Jimmy would just leave a voicemail, offering up an apology. Jimmy hated excuses, though, and the one he would use now placed the blame solely on the memory of his father. No way would Joey McSwain accept culpability in his son's failed relationship—with a guy, no less.

He called anyway. Voicemail again.

"Barry, hey, it's Jimmy. Look, uh, we should talk. I mean, really, I should talk and you should listen. I need to say I'm sorry," he said. "I'd like to. To your face. Call me. Or not. Be well. I enjoyed getting to know you."

He closed the phone just as the doors to the theatre opened, the sound of applause filling the lobby and wafting out into the street. Curious bypassers gawked inside to try and get a quick glimpse of the set, or maybe even a star taking his final bow. It took ten minutes, but at last the house cleared. Jimmy ducked his head inside, waved at his mother, who saw him and smiled as she said goodnight to the manager.

"Jimmy, that's sweet of you to pick up your mother," Stephanie said.

"I raised a good boy," Maggie said, grabbing hold of Jimmy's arm.

The two of them headed out, turned west, and crossed Eighth Avenue while tourists and locals alike battled it out for any available cabs. Sometimes it was nice to walk in New York, and with his mother at his side, he was reminded that this city was home, not a way of life most people in this country understood. Small apartments, no yards, tight sidewalks, cockroaches you wouldn't want to see in a dark alley, but it was all he knew. He embraced the energy of the city like he'd embraced Barry, with zeal, with passion, and always in his heart with a hint of regret. He didn't have the white picket fence, he didn't have the kids, the dog, the perky blonde wife. Life takes unexpected turns. Live it full or let it claim you.

As they hit Ninth Avenue, Jimmy asked his mother if she wanted to stop at Paddy's.

"Not tonight, honey. We've got the matinee tomorrow and an Actor's Fund at night."

"Ah, two-show Sunday. Got it."

He walked her to the building but not up those four flights of stairs, kissing her cheek on the stoop before they went their separate ways. She touched his unshaven cheek, held it there.

"You okay, Jim?"

"I'm fine, Ma."

"Mallory's case…how's it going?"

"Took a bad turn last night," he said.

"How bad?"

"The worst."

She knew what that meant, it was Jimmy-speak for death. "Anytime you want a spot on the aisle with me, just say so."

"Ma, you know I can't."

She patted his cheek again. "I know, you've always been independent."

Jimmy swallowed hard, thinking: Not always.

Maggie retired upstairs, and Jimmy started off down Tenth Avenue. He thought of going to Paddy's by himself, considered having a drink at Gaslight. It was a constant dual, his Irish roots and his gay identity. He had to wonder if he was not unlike Harris Rothschild, caught in a nexus of uncertainty, continually pulled in different directions.

These thoughts captured his attention, so much he wasn't paying attention to his surroundings.

He never made it to Paddy's or Gaslight.

He never saw the first punch coming, nor the second.

By the time the fourth one slammed hard into his face, he was down for the count.

Just blocks away, the harsh neon lights of Times Square blazed, immersing the dark night in the conflicting rays of daylight.

But for Jimmy McSwain, way west on Tenth Avenue, life went completely black.

CHAPTER ELEVEN

He'd lost a day.

Monday morning, more than thirty-six hours had slipped by since the attack, and Jimmy McSwain still woke with a throbbing headache. His puffy eyes opened on a blurry world, but he thought he detected a shadowy figure hovering over him, dancing across the slit of his eyes like the taunt of death. He blinked and it disappeared, not yet ready to claim him. He might be battered and bruised, but Jimmy would heal.

"Where am I?" he asked, his voice scratchy.

"Home."

His mother's voice, that much he recognized. A good sign, no permanent damage.

"Good, smells…sweet."

"Banana bread, your favorite."

"Thanks," he mumbled.

"I should have brought you to the hospital," she said.

"No," he said.

"That's what you said Saturday night and again Sunday afternoon."

"I did?"

"You don't remember?"

The fog was beginning to lift, replaced by dazed confusion. "Wait, what day is today?"

"Monday," she said. "Doc Hannigan stopped by a couple of times. He said you don't have a concussion. Otherwise you'd be in the emergency room, or worse."

Much as he didn't want to see what he looked like now, he didn't want to imagine worse. Jimmy attempted to sit up, but the headache throbbed so hard he thought his brain had fallen out. "Oww," was his next word, and its sound lingered, as did the pain. He felt like his limbs were on fire, the pain in his side intense. He tried to focus, to remember. He'd been walking down the street…

Nothing else came to mind.

He started to get up, felt his brain rattle again. "Aspirin," he said.

Maggie was ready with them, and he downed two along with a tall glass of water. The shocking cold felt good on his lips, like finding an oasis in the desert. As he stood, he turned and examined himself in the mirror that hung above the sofa. A purple version of his former face stared back. That's when he recalled the meaty punch that had come out of thin air, taking shape just as it slammed into him, and not just once. Repeatedly, until he had fallen to the hard ground, taking a brutal kick to the ribs before his body and mind shut down from the assault.

The kick. No wonder his side hurt. He was home, so his ribs must not be cracked.

"What does the other guy look like?" Jimmy asked.

"We don't know. He escaped."

"Yeah, apparently unscathed," his sister Meaghan said. "No way you would have been able to fight back. Whoever he was, he did you over good. Ronnie Gulliver found you on the steps leading to a basement apartment in his building. Heard you groaning."

He'd have to thank Ronnie, buy him a few rounds. He tried to speak, and in the end just accepted the icepack Meaghan had in her hand. He opted not to say anything to her, not because he couldn't handle her attitude and gum smacking, but because his mouth hurt. Not so surprising considering his lips were split and swollen, a large purple bruise on his cheek. As he attempted a smile, he felt his lip split further and tasted blood. At least he seemed to have all his teeth. Good. Nothing wrong with his smile that time couldn't fix.

"Meaghan, leave your brother alone."

"Fine, I'm going out. It's my day off anyway, don't need to play nursemaid."

Meaghan popped a bubble and then was gone, the apartment that much more quiet. Jimmy felt the headache lessen. He eased back down on the sofa, catching his head in his hands. He felt the rough stubble on his cheeks and figured it would be a few days before he could shave. Least of his troubles, he knew, but that's where his mind went. It was easier than having to deal with the truth. He'd been ambushed, and he didn't know why.

"You didn't call the cops, did you?" he asked Maggie.

She sat beside him, stretching a soothing arm across his shoulders. "I should have, but no. Ronnie called Uncle Paddy, who got a couple of the boys to fetch you and brought you home They said no police."

"Thanks, that was the right thing to do."

"No hospitals, no police. My Jimmy, independent to the end."

He tried to laugh but ended up coughing. "Well, it's not the end yet, Ma."

She playfully messed with his hair. "You need a haircut," she said.

That's when he knew he'd be fine. If Maggie McSwain could make light of his beating and instead comment on the mundane, then all was fine in the world. He promised her he would. "You know, before St. Patty's day."

She nodded, ruffled his hair again. "Coffee? Eggs? You got an appetite?"

He realized he was starving. "Sounds great. Plus a couple slices of toasted banana bread. I think I'll shower first."

Mother and son settled on their tasks, she to the kitchen while Jimmy padded down to the bathroom. In minutes he was beneath the hot spray, the water like pinpricks against his sensitive skin. He had a purple-colored bruise the size of Vermont on his left side where he'd taken the brunt of the guy's boot. Did he just assume that detail, or had he seen the tip of a boot coming at him? The image was blurry, like his vision, but something told him that's exactly what had happened. He soaped carefully because even bending down hurt. Afterwards, he dried off, slipped into his bedroom and donned a pair of shorts and a T-shirt. He felt refreshed, awake from the shower, and now the only thing washing over him was newfound determination. He'd canvass the neighborhood, ask questions of the people who lived around where he'd been attacked. Kind neighbors like Ronnie Gulliver looked out for each other here, blatant nosiness welcomed. Half of Hell's Kitchen was related, so it was family looking after family.

As he ate a plate of eggs and chomped on a couple of sausages, he checked his phone.

He had three missed calls and one broken screen.

Not much he could do about the latter issue right now. As to the former, he noticed that Harris Rothschild had phoned, as had Detective Roscoe Barone. The third call had been from Barry, and he was the only one not to leave a message. He'd deal with all of them soon enough. As he pushed aside his empty plate, he got up and kissed his mother on the cheek.

"Thanks, Ma, just what I needed."

"Where do you think you're going?"

He held up his phone. "I got some work to do."

"Jimmy, you need to rest. Let your body heal."

"Ma, I'm not sitting on the sofa and watching *The View* with you."

She knew how stubborn her son could be, so she let him go. He dressed a few minutes later and was out the door. He took the stairs lightly, feeling strength return to his legs with each step down. The bright sunshine and cold breeze hit him outside, fueling him, invigorating his body. Sunglasses helped with the glare, but he supposed he must look a fright with his bruises. Just don't walk past any schoolyards. No sense scaring the kids.

Normally, he'd walk. It was his favorite way around the city, but his body wasn't that much healed. He grabbed a cab, if only to avoid subway stares. As he traveled south, he opened up his phone and dialed. It took just one ring.

"Harris, it's Jimmy McSwain. Sorry not to call back sooner."

"It's fine. Uh, where are you?"

"On my way to see you, if that works. Are you at the club?"

"Upstairs in my apartment," he said.

"See you in ten."

It was closer to eight minutes; the traffic down Ninth was pretty light on this Monday. He was buzzed in, though it might not have been necessary as two men were just opening the first of the two doors of the front entrance. Seeing them in broad daylight, dressed in regular clothes, their appearance took him by surprise. He was fairly confident they were Cher and Cher Alike. They smiled at him and held the door even as it was being buzzed from upstairs, and when he stole a glance over their shoulder he found them staring back at him. Checking out his bruises, or his ass?

Forgetting them, he walked up the flight of stairs and heard the door open.

Harris was also in regular clothes, his face free of makeup. He was still beautiful.

Quite the opposite of Jimmy's appearance.

"Oh my God, what happened to you?"

"I fell on something."

"What?"

"Someone's fist. Several times."

"Come in, please…can I get you some ice for that bruise?"

"I think my face is still frozen from the ice pack my mother used all day yesterday."

"You mean, this didn't just happen?"

"Saturday night, not paying attention, thinking too much.

Wham, bam."

"And not the good kind."

"No thank you, ma'am," Jimmy replied. "So, how are you doing?"

"Kind of numb, still. Seems…unreal."

"Only one who knows the reality of death is the victim, I suppose."

Harris offered him a seat and Jimmy took it, figuring he'd get the rest when he could. Dashing off to the kitchen, Harris returned with two Cokes, set one before Jimmy. He took a grateful sip before setting it down. He found Harris staring at him. Might as well just plunge in.

"You spoke with your mother?"

"Spoke to her. I haven't seen her. I…I can't."

"What about the funeral?"

"Police haven't released the body yet, fortunately for me. So I don't have to decide yet."

"Whenever arrangements are made, don't miss it."

"I'm not so sure I can do that. The last image my father had of me was one that had me dressed as a woman. Now the man inside of me is supposed to go to his funeral and…what? Allow myself to see that last image of my father lying dead in a casket? Images neither one of us wanted."

"When it comes to the big issues, we hardly ever get to choose."

Harris seemed to mull over Jimmy's hard-earned wisdom. Jimmy was glad not to have to explain how he'd become so worldly.

"Let me ask you something, Harris. Your other…persona. Miss Jellicle Balls. Do you do it just as a job? Or is it more?"

"Far more than a job. It's who I am."

"A woman."

"Sometimes I feel that way…most times I do. Yes."

"So playing her on stage fuels some need you feel."

He looked away, as though the answer were hidden somewhere in the apartment. He focused again on the crack in the ceiling, like he'd slipped answers through it. When at last he faced Jimmy again, his eyes were ringed with tears. "Actually, Miss Jellicle Balls is helping me decide. About whether I want to be her…full time."

Jimmy had wondered about this. He hadn't wanted to be the one to bring it up. "A sex change, is that what you're referring to?"

He nodded. "Maybe. Terence is helping me."

"How?"

"The Dress Up Club, sure, it's a form of entertainment for the patrons. For us performers, though, it's a place to feel at home, a haven of sorts. Same with this building. Terence takes us in, gives us an apartment, sometimes alone, sometimes with a roommate, depending on whether he thinks we need someone around us. He helps us figure out what's best for each…tenant."

"He owns the entire building?"

"Terence made a fortune in real estate years ago. He lives on the top floor, but otherwise, yeah. The rest of them he makes available to those who come to him, usually by recommendation. Sometimes he sees a lost soul in the audience, like he did with me. He says it's his way to give back, helping the forgotten find themselves. He struggled for years with his own sexuality, and finally he just stopped caring what other people thought."

"So everyone who stays here…"

"He pays the rent. For some of them, he pays for their counseling."

"You?"

"Not yet. I mean, I can pay my own way, I got money when I turned twenty-one."

Jimmy nodded. "So, what, this is like a halfway house?"

"For men confused about their sexuality or their identity. Freedom lives here."

Jimmy nodded.

"Sounds great. You're lucky to have found it, all of you are. Terry Cloth keeps impressing me. He's a lot of bluster, but I'm guessing much of that is an act. He's more than the mother hen he claimed."

"She likes you, too. Probably would like you even more if she saw you now."

"Right, I'm such a looker right now. Some tough guy."

Harris laughed. "See, that's the beauty of a man like Terence, he sees deeper."

Jimmy finished his Coke, and the conversation lagged suddenly. He rose from the sofa and said he had another appointment to get to. Harris seemed to accept the abrupt departure, but not before he thanked Jimmy, not just for letting him talk, but for the comfort he was providing for his mother.

"I can't do it all," Jimmy advised. "Just like sons need their fathers, mothers need their sons."

Harris understood, nodding as he opened the door. Before Jimmy departed, he realized he had one last question.

"Sure, shoot," Harris said.

Bad choice of words, but it helped with the transition. "Exactly what I want to talk about. Who do you think wanted your father dead?"

"My father wasn't a likable man. He intimidated people, and he made them feel inferior."

"Not exactly a motive for murder."

"I'm sure he had his enemies, Jimmy. I know it. Former clients, people he worked with and let go. When he fired someone, he didn't just want them gone, he wanted them destroyed."

"What about your mother?"

"What about her?"

"Did she hate him?"

Harris shook his head. "I don't know why, but she adored him. She wouldn't kill him."

Jimmy nodded. "Still, it doesn't seem like a professional hit. His death was personal, familial."

Harris looked away. "Why do you say that?"

"Think of the timing, shot dead right after a confrontation with you."

It was a comment neither of them had an answer to.

§ § §

His second call went straight to voicemail. Detective Barone must be out working a case or maybe in the men's room ridding his body of its noontime beer. He left a message saying he was returning the call, hailed a cab on the corner and journeyed back up Tenth Avenue. The phone felt hot in his hands, knowing he had a third call to return. He wondered what Barry had to say to him. He imagined an awkward conversation. He slipped the phone inside his jacket pocket, deciding it could wait.

When they came to the corner of 47th Street, Jimmy told the cabbie to pull over.

He paid the fare, got out, and made his way down the familiar sidewalk. Sunlight shined bright on its surface, highlighting dog poop some careless owner hadn't picked up. Shame, it took just one asshole to mar an otherwise lovely day. As he walked toward Ninth, he stopped at the spot he'd been Saturday night. He turned around just as he saw a bicyclist swish past him, and he heard the joyful squeal of a little girl playing across the street. A dog barked, and he wondered if that was the same dog who'd left shit on the curb. The sights and sounds of everyday life swirled around him, just like it was supposed to be. Normal. The sun bringing it all to vibrant life. Unlike the night, when shadows crept up on you, when violence lived. Taking you down a flight of steps, beating you bloody, kicking you until you passed out.

Jimmy examined the ground around his neighbor's building.

He peered down the iron steps that led to a basement apartment, where he'd been found. He didn't feel like venturing down there right now. He reminded himself he had to thank Ronnie.

But all that would wait. He would worry about his own case later. He was on the clock for Jellison Rothschild.

Reaching again for his phone, he typed out a quick text: HAD LUNCH YET?

He waited a beat and heard back. NO.

A moment later Mallory rang his phone. Texting wasn't her favorite form of communication, unlike Meaghan who lived by her lower case words. Phone calls took up more time, and as a lawyer, she'd been well trained in the fine art of billable hours.

"Where are you?" she asked.

He gazed around. "Scene of the crime."

"Yours or Saul's?"

"Actually, I've been at both already. Now mine."

"Ouch. You feel up to meeting me?"

"Tell me when."

"Fifteen minutes, my building's lobby. My treat."

"You'll get off easy, not sure how much I can chew."

She laughed. "Poor, Jimmy."

He closed the phone and stared at it, thinking he should return that last call to Barry.

He put his personal life on hold, and even though he was meeting his sister for lunch, it was going to be all business. He was curious about Rothschild's so-called enemies, those who he had wronged.

Turned out Mallory was curious too, but about an entirely different topic.

CHAPTER TWELVE

"So, who's Barry?" Mallory asked the moment they sat down and drinks were set before them.

She had iced tea; Jimmy had a glass of red wine. It was a fancy Italian restaurant just off Madison Avenue in the Fifties and Jimmy had supposed beer would be too west side. He sipped his wine and put up his pinky finger just to fit in.

"Ha-ha, funny, Jim. But you can't avoid the question."

"How do you know there even is a Barry?"

"Do you remember me being at Ma's yesterday?"

"Uh, sort of?"

"Man, you really got your clock cleaned, didn't you?"

"Guess so, lost some time."

She smiled at they way he kept the metaphor going. Mallory had a soothing way about her. She'd always been a typical oldest child, looking out for her two younger siblings with a fierce protectiveness, more paternal in her approach than maternal. And why not? She'd known Joey McSwain the longest of the siblings. She knew how he would have reacted to and handled certain situations like fights with bullies, teasing, the usual teenage crap. She'd stepped in often and effectively. She'd been less successful with the headstrong, impulsive, and defiant Meaghan. The girl just would not listen to anybody, not even her mother. With Jimmy, Mallory had once told him she sensed a more kindred spirit, and knew that underneath his tough exterior, a broken sensitivity lived. She was the first person Jimmy had ever come out to. Her response, "Yeah, Jim, I know. It's cool, it's fine. Just be happy." Nice if everyone reacted that way.

So when she grilled him about Barry, it was with a mixture of supportive sister and courtroom trickery.

"I almost picked up the call when I saw the name," she said.

"Thought he should know what's going on, even if he doesn't know me from Adam. I'm guessing he knows you."

"No comment. I'm glad you didn't pick up. He's not involved."

"Have you told him what happened? And, by the way, you look awful."

He drank more wine, feeling the sting of the alcohol as it hit his split lip. "Thanks, and no," he said, answering her in reverse. "Barry is just a guy…it's probably over anyway, really before it got a chance to be anything."

"What happened?"

"Me," he said.

"You shut him out."

"It was too soon, you know, to burden him with my issues."

"But not too soon you couldn't sleep with him?"

Mallory had a way to cutting to the heart of the matter, even while not judging. "I met him last week…exactly a week ago, Monday night."

"And it's already over? Wow, even for you that one was fast."

Fortunately, they were interrupted by the arrival of the waiter, a handsome redhead with a penchant for pointing. He read off the specials while punctuating the air with his index finger for emphasis when he particularly liked a dish. Mallory went with the risotto with asparagus and mushroom special. Jimmy, keeping his sore jaw in mind, ordered a simple plate of pasta with olive oil and garlic. The waiter tossed Jimmy a look of displeasure, making him wonder if it was because he'd ordered off the set menu after rattling on for two minutes about the specials, or because he was having red wine with a lighter sauce.

"I think it's because you didn't bat your eyes at him," Mallory suggested.

"Please, last thing I need is more relationship drama. Plus…"

"Yeah, I know, you don't like redheads," she said, with an easy laugh. "Okay, indulge me one last personal question, then I'll leave you alone and we can get down to business."

"Gee, can't wait."

"Are you ever going to get over Remy?"

Jimmy heard her question to the point that it rattled inside his already addled brain. He was tired of his sisters always bringing him up. Couldn't they stop opening up a wound that wouldn't heal? "So, how are things at the firm, given the events of the weekend?"

"Fine, change the subject. But just hear me out: you keep Remy in your heart, and no one else will be able to get anywhere near it. No need to respond, just give it some thought." She let silence linger as she drank her iced tea. "The office has been hell this morning because of shock and dismay over Saul's death. We had a staff meeting, and they even offered to spring for a counselor to come in and talk to us. We voted that one down. We lawyers are a tough breed. We'll deal with it in private. Still, I was glad to get out of there for an hour."

"Have the police visited the office yet?"

"From what the partners said, the police spoke to them on Sunday. If it's decided a more thorough interrogation of staff needs to be done, they'll be in touch."

"Now that you've had time to digest it, what's your theory?"

"Three a.m., rich guy. Wrong time, wrong place."

Jimmy supposed that could be the case. Or not. "He wasn't robbed, Saul still had his wallet on him. Full of cash."

"Shooter got scared. Maybe he didn't mean to pull the trigger. Just threaten him."

Jimmy nodded. "Could be. You don't think it was premeditated?"

"A killer following Saul Rothschild out at that hour of the night? It wasn't exactly Saul's pattern to go out like that. Why would someone even lie in wait thinking it was a possibility?"

"Good point," Jimmy said.

Their meals arrived, and Jimmy and Mallory dug in. With all this talk of murder and gun shots, he was glad not to have ordered the Bolognese. They talked as they dined. Mallory regaled Jimmy with stories of Saul Rothschild as a boss and mentor. He was fair, she said, but expected hard work, long hours, and true dedication. "And for the past seven years, that's exactly what he got from me. Now I don't know what tomorrow holds. Do I get to work with another of the partners, or does Saul's team get disbanded?"

"Surely they wouldn't fire you," he said.

"Doubt it. I bill too much."

Jimmy wiped sauce from his face, realizing the food was making him feel human again. Sharing a meal with his sister, indulging in a glass of wine, it all felt rather civilized, a far cry from the zany world of the Dress Up Club. For a moment, he imagined it wasn't Mallory sitting across from him but Barry, and the two of them were holding hands in anticipation of a night when they would allow their passions to explode. A time when they had worked through issues and could just enjoy the good part of a relationship. Jimmy blinked, looked up and rather than Barry, rather than his sister, he saw Remy. He could hear his accent, hear the regret tinged in his throat as he told Jimmy being together was impossible. Pain struck at Jimmy's heart, far worse than any physical soreness he'd endured Saturday night.

"Uh, hey…Jim, you still with me?"

He shook his head when he realized he'd been staring ahead. His glass hovered in front of him, the swirl of the wine washing away the images of nine months ago, when Remy St. Claire had walked out of his life. "Yeah, sorry, just zoned out I guess."

"You sure you don't have a concussion?"

"No, I'm thick-headed."

She raised her glass in the air. "You got that right, brother."

§ § §

Lunch over, Jimmy walked Mallory back to the office, kissed her cheek and thanked her.

"See you at dinner tonight," she reminded him.

Of course, it was Monday. Dinner with Ma.

So he had the whole afternoon to himself, and he pondered what he could do. Roscoe had yet to return his call, and he thought about going over to the precinct to nose around, but another idea hit him instead. He hopped on the 6 train at Lexington and 51st Street, transferred at Grand Central to the 4 express and rode it until the train rattled into the station at Atlantic Avenue/Barclays Center. Brooklyn again. As he went topside, he caught curious looks from the denizens of the downtown area and flipped on his sunglasses to avoid their stares. He was starting to forget that he looked like ground beef, but leave it to New Yorkers to remind him. No concern for his well-being, just a detached interest.

He found Montague Street and began the trek down to Eammon's Pub.

Ralphie was sitting at the bar, just like last week.

Jimmy pulled up a stool right beside him, ordered a Smithwick's. The sound of his voice made the old guy look his way.

"Back again, are ya? What, you got one of those unlimited Metrocards, taking the transit authority for all its worth?"

"Something like that," Jimmy said.

"You look like crap," Ralphie said, taking a pull on his Budweiser.

"Got stupid, someone jumped me."

"Random or a case?"

"Still not sure yet."

Ralphie nodded. "Walk the line between law and the unlawful, you gotta take your licks."

Jimmy's beer arrived. Ralphie told him to enjoy it, no rush. He wasn't in the mood for a walk along the concrete promenade. The way he was feeling today it might just as soon be a walk among the granite tombstones. Jimmy told him he was a long way from that and while Ralphie coughed his way through his ornery response, a pang hit Jimmy's chest, a tightness that had him wishing people could live forever. Ralphie had always been there for him over the years, helping set him up with the private investigator he trained under until he could strike out on his own. If not for Ralphie, Jimmy might just be the cop he didn't want to be. The idea he might one day get sick and disappear from his life was almost too much to consider, especially this time of year when loss breezed through the wind.

"What can I do for you?"

"You know a guy named Frisano?"

Ralphie paused, his beer stuck at his lips. "Fast-Track Frisano."

"So I hear. Ambitious guy?"

"Very. Moved up quick. Smart man. His record at Brooklyn's 71st was sterling."

"Manhattan, though, that's the grail."

"One Police Plaza someday, maybe Commish. Wouldn't that be something?"

Jimmy didn't know enough about Frisano to agree or not. "He approachable?"

"What do you want with Frisano?"

"I'm working a case, the same one as last week…it got ugly."

"Ugly mean deadly?"

Jimmy explained his client getting shot, and Ralphie listened to the details like the seasoned vet he was. Never knew if a kernel of truth existed among the supposition. "Do you think I'm losing my touch, Ralphie? I mean, a client was having me followed, and I didn't even pick up on it. Hell, I didn't even suspect it. What the hell's up with that?"

"Says more about your client's paranoia than it does your investigative skills," Ralphie stated matter-of-factly. It was the sensibility only years on the job could get you. You never could know enough when you needed it. Only hindsight had twenty-

twenty vision. "Rich man caught you unaware. Location does that."

"What do you mean?"

"Wealthy Upper East Siders, they hire you to find their spoiled son. You probably had it pegged as an easy case, no danger."

Jimmy had to admit the old cop was right.

"So, the widow wants you to find out what happened."

"But Roscoe and Dean haven't given me much. Roscoe called me yesterday when I was kind of out of it. I called back this morning, got his voicemail. No return call so far. I'm not sure what he wants. Maybe just to tell me to butt out."

"So you figure to call on Frisano?"

"Might as well get to know the new captain, right? I've had a bunch of cases in Chelsea."

"I can make a call," Ralphie said.

"Thanks. I appreciate it. Next one's on me."

Ralphie nodded, finished the beer in his hand and signaled for another. The bartender had it served up fast, and Ralphie took his first sip like it was nectar of the Gods. Another of those regretful pangs hit Jimmy, realizing that this was the old man's life now. He was widowed and he'd never had any kids, so who cared for him when he needed it? Jimmy, sure, he'd do anything for him, but he'd probably hear of Ralphie's death before he'd even know he was sick. That's just how he was, old school, pride before dependency.

"So, you still like boys?" Ralphie asked.

Jimmy just laughed. "Yeah, Ralphie, nothing's changed."

"Hell, everything changed. My world is gone, kid. It's moved beyond me."

Jimmy let the remark go, and the two men sat in companionable silence, watching a Mets spring training game on the television. They were playing the Marlins and were down 5-2. By the time the seventh inning arrived and they were down 12-3, Jimmy decided it was his turn to stretch, so he drained his beer, thanked Ralphie for doing what he could with Frisano, and made his way back into the sunshine after paying the tab. He donned his sunglasses again and strolled down to the Brooklyn Heights promenade anyway.

Leaning against the railing, he stared at the always-impressive Manhattan skyline. Despite the overwhelming sight of steel and glass, man-made structures that towered high, none were a match for the blue sky that stretched on forever. Nature still won out.

He knew he was expected at his mother's later, and it was probably better to get a move on before rush hour hit the subways, and he was packed in like a sardine without oil. He started back when he heard his phone ring. He grabbed for it, wondering if Ralphie had already pulled strings and arranged for an audience with this hot shot rising star of the NYPD.

It wasn't Ralphie calling.

It was Barry.

He almost didn't pick it up. Was he ready for conversation? He liked the embrace of silence.

"This is Jimmy," he finally said.

"Hi…it's…"

"I know. Hi, Barry."

"Sorry, if you're busy, but…"

"It's okay. I'm free. I owed you a call. I still owe you something more."

"You okay? You sound distant."

"I'm outside, near the water. Maybe you hear the wind."

"Oh, yeah, sure."

"Barry, it's okay, you can ask."

Prompted, Barry didn't hold back. "What happened that night?"

"Life, Barry. People are imperfect, people have flaws."

"You turned dark so fast. It was a side of you I didn't like."

"Get in line," was Jimmy's flippant response, which he regretted the moment it was out.

"Yeah, see, that's what I can't handle. Maybe we should, you know, say good-bye."

The idea of saying good-bye so quickly seemed so wrong, a chance at something meaningful taken away. What about the attraction between them? How could it have burned out so fast? The way Barry kissed him, his lips on his throat, licking at the nape in his neck, his clinging embrace while they made love, darkness swirling around them even as lights exploded inside their minds. The way they lay at peace together afterwards, touching and caressing, the expression of satisfaction in their eyes. Could it all be gone with the simple word of good-bye?

"That what you want?"

"I don't know."

"Let's not do this over the phone," Jimmy said.

A pause, which could mean Barry was considering the suggestion of perhaps not quite a date, but a get-together. "Look, I've got a meeting in five minutes, let me think about it, I'll call you tonight. Maybe that's poetic, our anniversary."

The word struck at Jimmy gut. Anniversaries to him were sad occasions.

"I'm sorry, what?"

"A week. I know, it's silly to think that way. Sorry, I'll call you later."

Jimmy said okay, and what he heard next was dead air. As though the connection between two people could be cut so quickly. Not unlike how the blast of a gun could forever undo the bond between father and son.

CHAPTER THIRTEEN

Jimmy slept at his mother's Monday night, in his own bed rather than on the sofa, a sure sign he was nearly back to full strength. The bruises on his body would fade eventually, but the hurt was gone, aided partly by his mother's pre-St. Patrick's Day corned beef and cabbage but more so by the late-night phone conversation he'd had with Barry, in which they had agreed to meet up on Wednesday night.

"To talk," Barry had stated with an undercurrent to his words: verbal intercourse, not the other kind.

Still, the mere fact Barry was giving him a second chance warmed his heart, and so it was with a rare smile Jimmy slept, the good mood continuing into the next morning when his phone buzzed and stirred him from the deep slumber his achy body craved.

"This is Jimmy," he said, his voice groggy.

"You went over my head."

Thank goodness for caller I.D., forewarning Jimmy of the quiet wrath of Detective Roscoe Barone. He shook the sleep from his eyes and focused on the new day and this new development.

"Thought I should meet the new Captain."

"Yeah, well, lucky you, McSwain. The wizard has granted you an audience. Ten o'clock this morning. Don't be late. And don't expect him to send you home to Kansas too quickly."

"Really, Roscoe, a Wizard of Oz reference? Isn't that my territory?"

"Just want to make you comfortable. Like I said, don't be late. Dorothy."

Roscoe hung up, so did Jimmy and by nine forty-five on one of those dreary, overcast days where rain threatened but didn't fall, he found himself walking through the doors of the 10th

Precinct. Temperature was a raw thirty-four, so he had donned one of his leather jackets. He had on jeans and a button-down shirt with a black T-shirt under it, his version of dressing up for the occasion. With the bruises on his face fading, he'd even braved shaving, launching an early morning interrogation from his mother of what the special occasion was. It took all his efforts to convince her he was just meeting with the cops.

"Well, look what the cat dragged in," Jimmy heard as he approached the dispatch desk.

"That line sounds familiar," he told Wren Parker.

"If it works, I say stick with it."

"Meow," he said.

"No, Jim, you're what the cat…oh, never mind. Have a seat. The Wizard's not in yet."

"You know why I'm here?"

"We're cops, Jimmy, we know everything."

"Where's Jimmy Hoffa buried?"

She frowned at him, even though he could tell she was amused. "The way you look now, lucky you we're not asking who tried to kill Jimmy McSwain."

So the thankfully-alive Jimmy stayed put while Wren went back to her desk duties, and he helped himself to a cup of uninspired coffee from the machine in the corner. He studied the "Wanted" posters on the bulletin board, none of the sought-after perps looking familiar. Again, the thought occurred that the attack on him last Saturday might have been random. Plenty of guys on the streets of New York were an eight ball short of a pool game. But whoever had nearly made ground beef out of him had to take a back seat, because a piece of high-grade sirloin had just made its way into the precinct.

Jimmy noticed the difference immediately. Wren stood taller, the chatty nonsense coming from the other cops came to a stop, and everyone suddenly was as busy as could be. The new captain in town, one F.X. Frisano, walked into the main squad room, announcing his presence with a friendly wave. "Morning, troops. It's a gonna be another bad day to be a bad guy."

Not a bad rally cry, Jimmy thought.

Frisano was about thirty-five, with dark, slick swept-back hair. His crisp uniform was deep blue, the gold bars on his shoulders shiny like he'd just been handed them. He was a man who cared about his appearance, but it wasn't so much the uniform as the body beneath it. The guy was cut. He filled out the material perfectly, and to top it all off, Jimmy couldn't help but notice the man was strikingly attractive. Deep olive skin tones, the shadow of his beard so heavy he'd always have a hint of stubble even if he had shaved two hours ago. But his dark eyes truly captured Jimmy's attention, drawn into their universe the moment they landed on him. Simply put, F.X. Frisano was sexy hot.

Was it wrong that Jimmy McSwain was hugely attracted to him?

Yeah. At the moment, it was.

This wasn't Gaslight, and it wasn't Musical Mondays. He was no Officer Krupke.

"You must be Jimmy McSwain," Frisano said, approaching him.

"Your detective skills need no sharpening," Jimmy responded, extending his hand.

Frisano hesitated, his face just inches from Jimmy's, before accepting the proffered handshake. Sudden electricity sizzled in the air as the two men's hands connected. Their eyes remained locked on each other, almost like they were playing that childhood game of who would blink first. This was no game. One man was marking his territory while the other showed no sign of being intimidated.

Jimmy had to wonder which was which.

At last the handshake ended and Frisano said, "Follow me, Jim."

Jim. So casual, like they were suddenly best friends. It was a good move on Frisano's part, potentially disarming if Jimmy wasn't already attuned to the sneaky interrogation technique. Not quite good cop since he had no one to play off of. Still, Jimmy found himself following in the hot captain's wake. Frisano had a nice, tight ass, but Jimmy reminded himself to focus on the case and not let this dizzying sense of attraction distract him.

He was led into an interrogation room, the white walls bare, one side with an observation window. Frisano announced he'd be back in a few minutes, leaving Jimmy to his own devices, except for the fact he was probably under surveillance from behind that glassed window. He waved, mouthed the words "Hey, Roscoe," then settled down in a chair with a grin. He knew the drill.

It was more like thirty minutes until Frisano returned, not bad considering this was all a big power play. Had Jimmy been a suspect, the wait could have been an hour or more. When Frisano finally returned, he wasn't alone. Lieutenants Roscoe Barone and Larry Dean walked in behind him. New friend, old friend, one-time childhood chum, all of them now part of a tight brotherhood that Jimmy had once seen betray his family.

"Is it a good day to be a private investigator?" Jimmy asked.

Frisano closed the door. None of them laughed.

§ § §

"Tell me about Saul Rothschild."

That's how it began, no warm-up, no prelude.

"He's dead," Jimmy said.

"Good, you read the papers. Now tell me how you came to be involved with him."

Frisano sat on the edge of the desk, hovering over Jimmy. Dean sat backwards in another chair to help even the playing field and establish a comfort level, while Roscoe stood in the corner, arms crossed and a stern expression on his ruddy face. Power positions established, all that remained were the questions and answers.

So Jimmy spilled what he could. His sister, Mallory, worked

for Rothschild's firm. He wanted to hire a private investigator for a personal matter, and she recommended her brother because that's what he did for a living. The meeting at the apartment, the fancy luncheon, Rothschild's apparent disapproval of his son's sexual orientation, the private chat with Jellison, the almost too-easy way he'd tracked down Harris. It didn't take long to fill in those details, mostly because Frisano just listened. He nodded all the while, encouraging Jimmy to continue, not once interrupting. His summary ended with Harris's call in the middle of the night.

"That's where you guys entered the picture," Jimmy concluded.

"Except you left out the part where the widow hired you to find the killer."

"I didn't leave it out. Roscoe and Dean already knew. I figured that meant you did."

"Don't concern yourself with what you think we know, McSwain."

Ah, no more Jim, he noted.

"Sure, Jellison Rothschild hired me. Is that why you called me, Roscoe? To warn me off the case?"

Rosoce kept his arms crossed, his expression answer enough.

Frisano continued the verbal volley. "And yesterday you were seen visiting the offices of Rothschild's firm."

"I never made it past the lobby," he clarified. "Like I said, my sister works there. She took me to lunch."

"You had the spaghetti," Frisano said.

"With an olive oil and garlic sauce," Jimmy confirmed, nonplussed by what they knew.

"My mother makes the best red gravy ever," Frisano said.

Typical Brooklyn Italian, Jimmy thought. Nothing but red sauce on your pasta.

"My mother's specialty is corned beef and cabbage. We had it last night."

Roscoe and Dean gave each other curious looks, but Frisano

stayed focused on Jimmy.

"We want to show you something," he said.

"Sure."

Frisano nodded at Dean, the low-man on the totem pole. He disappeared from the room and returned with a laptop, already fired up and ready. He pressed the mouse and a fuzzy image came into focus. The familiar scene was Tenth Avenue, right outside the Dress Up Club. A neighborhood surveillance camera footage played, and Jimmy could discern the time and date from the digital display at the lower right part of the screen. He looked at Frisano for a second, the Captain's eyes directing him back to the screen. Just as he did, he saw a figure emerge into the camera's view. Jimmy recognized his client, Saul Rothschild, and based on his body language, he wasn't very happy. He was storming up the street, no doubt angry over his confrontation with his son. Just then a second figure could be seen, his arm jutting out from a darkened storefront. The fiery blast happened a second later, and Rothschild crumbled to the ground, the gun following suit. The assailant stood, hovered, looked around, and then ran. He was gone from sight almost faster than the bullet had left the gun.

Jimmy blanched, even knowing what he would be witnessing.

Not like a movie or television show, this wasn't an actor being fired upon by a blank. The damage done here was real, permanent, and for Jimmy McSwain, seeing a man gunned down with no forewarning took him back fifteen years. He hoped that Harris would not be subjected to watching this. A son, no matter his age, no matter how strong he was, should not watch his own father die like that, even in a recording.

At last, Jimmy spoke. "Any leads on the perp?"

Frisano shook his head. "Wish that were the case."

"You can't see the guy's face."

"He's wearing one of those hoodies. Trying to look all street."

"Trying?" Jimmy asked. "Meaning it was a guise."

Frisano looked over at Dean, who then zoomed in on the

image of the assailant. The shot focused on the man's wrist, Jimmy's eye first going to the gun. But the gun wasn't the important part, because he knew the cops had retrieved it at the scene after it had been dropped. What caught his attention was a shiny metal object, and he leaned in closer to the pixilated screen, examining it.

"A watch," Jimmy said.

"Good eye. What else can you tell me about it?"

"Looks expensive."

"It's a gold Rolex," said Roscoe, stepping forward. "We showed a screen shot of it to a local jeweler, and he identified it immediately. Doesn't know the model because the picture's not clear enough. But he recognized certain attributes to be ninety-nine percent certain."

"Your everyday thug doesn't wear such a watch," Jimmy said, "unless he'd just robbed someone else."

"Right, but if he's a common street thug out for a night of crime, why not steal the wallet off the dead guy?" Frisano said. "We found it inside his jacket pocket. Turns out Rothschild had over two thousand bucks in his wallet."

An excellent point, and a good piece of detection. "Bribe money?"

"Interesting theory. For some people, that's a lot of cash."

"Not for Rothschild. Could have just been his usual carrying around money."

"True," Frisano said. "Regardless of how much the vic was carrying, it clearly didn't interest the killer. Money wasn't his motive."

"A revenge killing," Jimmy said, "which goes to the idea of premeditation."

"Boys, give our private eye a passing grade," Frisano said.

Frisano's comment was both complimentary and derisive. Jimmy thought it was his first misstep, because as friendly and open as the police had been in their investigation, the remark served as a reminder that Jimmy, despite being on their side when it came to battling the so-called bad guys, was still an independent operator and, thus, a thorn in their side.

Frisano pushed forward. "You say Rothschild had you followed."

"That's the logical explanation. I have it from both the son and the wife that he had trust issues, and that he was using me to find his son, ready to step in and handle the situation the moment I'd found him. Looks like that's what happened. So yeah, he had someone watch my every move. Once I'd located Harris, he came in fast and took over. Didn't end well."

"And in a curious case of irony, someone seemed to be following him."

Jimmy nodded. "Let me see that footage again."

Dean replayed it, Jimmy zeroing in on the wrist with the watch around it.

"Tell me what you're thinking," Frisano said.

"Thinking maybe it could be a woman. But it's not. Too thick."

"You thinking the wife did it? Angry because of the way he treated their son?"

Jimmy wouldn't like to think of Jellison as a killer. But he'd seen worse performances.

"Imagine, her husband hires a private eye. She hires a killer."

Jimmy nodded. "They certainly had different parenting styles when it came to Harris."

"We released the body to the family," Frisano said. "Funeral in a few days."

"I'll be there," Jimmy said.

"That's what we were hoping. Stay alert, report back."

It was a signal that their interrogation had come to an end, with Dean taking command of the laptop, leaving the room. Roscoe shook Jimmy's hand, said thanks for his cooperation, which was magnanimous of the old school cop, acknowledging that Jimmy might have been helpful already and could still prove to be. Then he stepped out of the room, leaving Jimmy alone with Frisano.

"I'll walk you out," the Captain said.

An interesting move that made Jimmy both wary and curious.

Frisano's staff came to attention just as before. When they emerged into the fresh air, rain had begun to fall, dotting the sidewalks with small drops that wouldn't soak a cat, but enough of a gray pallor to keep the mood focused on murder.

"Something else I can do for you, Captain?"

"Outside these doors, you can call me Frank."

"Okay," Jimmy said.

"Francis Xavier Frisano," he said.

"That's a mouthful."

"Irish mother, Italian father."

"You said she cooks the best red gravy."

"She learned from her mother-in-law."

Jimmy nodded, wondering what the point of all this was. Frisano forged ahead.

"I read up about you. You went through the academy but never took the oath."

"I wanted the training, not the badge."

"A crusader against crime, notably guns."

"I don't like guns."

Frisano nodded and looked up at the sky. Jimmy's eyes followed, because that's what being in this man's presence made you do. Whatever he did, you did. Raindrops fell into his eyes, and Jimmy blinked, the drops now like tears down his cheeks.

"I know about your father. Good cop, cut down way too early."

Jimmy wiped away those rain-induced tears. "No argument

there."

"Dean filled in the rest," he said.

"Neighborhood kids. He was a couple years ahead of me."

"He says you're good but maybe too emotional when it comes to cases."

"Like I said, I don't like guns. I don't approve of violence. I like to stop it."

It was at that point that Frisano put his hand on Jimmy's shoulder. "I don't like unsolved cases."

"I'll help all I can to put Rothschild's in the books."

"Good. But that's not what I meant."

Jimmy's pulse raced. Where was Frisano going with this?

"We call them cold cases."

"Everyone knows that. They even had a TV show called that."

"I hate cold cases. It means the cops didn't do their job first time around."

Jimmy wasn't about to protest that. He'd heard the lame excuses when he was fourteen.

"Dean says you won't rest until your father's killer is caught."

"Guess it's my life's work. It motivates me in my cases. I hate seeing others go through what I did."

"Like Harris Rothschild."

"Yes, he witnessed his father's murder, too."

"So this case, it's personal."

"Is that a bad thing?"

"No, we need your drive, your determination. Cops have to maintain distance."

"So I'm like a movie tagline, 'this time it's personal'?"

Frisano nodded, extending his hand once more. Jimmy shook it, feeling that same driving heat as before. He stared into Frisano's dark eyes, unsure of what to read in them. Stone-faced, he gave little away. Jimmy supposed that's how he'd progressed so far up the blue ladder so fast. At last they parted ways, and Frisano started back inside the precinct. He turned back, one thing still unsaid between them.

"I'm looking forward to working with you, Jim."

"Thanks, Frank. Me, too."

Frisano went behind closed doors, back into his world of procedures and rules.

Jimmy started off down the street, the rain increasing with each step.

But he didn't even notice getting wet, because he was busy wondering why Ralphie had left out one crucial detail about the man some called The Wizard, others called Fast-Track Frisano. Francis Xavier Frisano, the hot new captain of Chelsea's 10th Precinct was gay. And attracted to Jimmy.

The feeling was mutual.

CHAPTER FOURTEEN

Three days until the fifteenth anniversary of his father's murder, a rainy Tuesday night found Jimmy sitting in his office, poring over old files relating to his father's unsolved case. Frisano's words rang in his mind, and he realized that perhaps for the first time in his life he had a true ally within the police department, one who understood what motivated him. What he didn't know was Frisano's story—what drove him to over-achieve. He'd mentioned his mother but his father only in passing. Did he have some issue there, perhaps pertaining to Frank's sexuality? Such answers would have to wait for another time.

Sitting on the floor in front of the sofa, the files spread out before him, Jimmy picked up a yellowed article from the *Post*. It hadn't been front-page news back then, thankfully, but page four carried the sordid details. He read them silently, his lips moving from memory. How often had he read this piece wishing it were fiction? A cop thriller where the happy ending was only three hundred pages away, not a cliffhanger that left the reader emotionally cheated. The photograph that accompanied the article was his father's official NYPD portrait, one of their finest in one his proudest shots—his dress blue cap, the curious eyes beneath it, the thick bristly mustache as distinctive to Joey McSwain as was his walk or his gruff, gravelly voice that could be softened with a stern look from his wife.

He ran a finger over the photograph, smoothing away an aged crinkle in the paper.

He never talked to his father in the photo; he just looked, he studied, he stared.

And he vowed, silently, to put his memory to rest.

He moved on to the copies of the police report filed by the first responders. He never tired of the details, believing one day a clue would reveal itself to him. Two punks, he read, argued at a deli, one ran off after robbing the place, Joey McSwain, officially off duty but always wearing the badge, chased after him and took a simple bullet to the forehead. He dropped to the ground, he died as the blood spilled out of him, staining the clothes of McSwain's fourteen-year-old son, who clutched at his dying father. The prose was very matter-of-fact, by-the-books, clinical. What it failed to mention was the stain that continued to spread, from his clothes to his heart, and even deeper.

Taking a pull on the warm Yuengling by his side, Jimmy was about to close up the files when his cell phone buzzed. Setting the bottle down, he saw the caller I.D. and picked up.

"Mrs. Rothschild."

"I'm downstairs," she said.

"Excuse me? Downstairs where?"

"In front of your building. You address is on your business card."

"I'll come down, let's grab a drink at Paddy's."

"I'd rather speak privately, Jimmy."

He looked around at the mess on the floor. He'd have to clean up. What was laid out was for his eyes only. "Okay, give me a minute, and I'll buzz you up."

"Now, please. It's raining something fierce."

So he pressed the buzzer and heard the door click open downstairs. Dressed in just a pair of shorts, he realized cleaning up the files on the floor would have to take a backseat to his looking professional. Grabbing his blue jeans from the back of a chair, he slipped them on and shrugged into a nearby sweater, his head poking out just as she knocked at the door. So much for socks and shoes. He padded barefoot to the door, opened it, and let in a frazzled Jellison Rothschild, her eyes darting about. She was wrapped in a long dark raincoat, her hair protected by a matching hat. He didn't notice an umbrella. No doubt she'd taken a cab.

"Come in. Sorry about the mess."

"No apologies needed," she said. "A man who lives alone and

does what you do for a living, I wasn't expecting champagne and caviar and floral prints."

People had a way of assigning their own contexts to other's situations.

"May I get you a drink?"

"What do you have?"

He admitted all that was in his refrigerator was a six-pack, currently down to five.

"I don't really live here, just...."

"Entertain?" she asked naughtily, arching her finely-drawn eyebrow. For a moment he saw not her, but her son doing his impersonation of her.

"I work on cases here."

"Is that what that is on the floor...one of your cases?"

He nodded, wishing he'd had time to put it all away. "Let's talk about yours."

She settled on the chair at his desk, shedding her coat. Jimmy hung it in the closet. When he turned around, he saw that she wore a simple black dress. She was still in mourning, but even so, her makeup was flawless, her hair like she'd just come from the salon. As she crossed her legs, Jimmy was reminded of how much younger she had been than Saul. All that she lacked was a cigarette, and she could have been the classic damsel in distress, circa 1950.

"I'll take that beer," she said. "I think I need it."

On his way to the small kitchen, Jimmy grabbed his bottle off the floor and set it on the counter. He grabbed two cold bottles, twisted the caps and hastily returned to the main room. Jellison accepted it, took a pull on it like a pro. Clearly she had a past that didn't teach you what fork to use or what wine went with what meal. Jimmy settled on the edge of the sofa, facing her.

"The police tell me they've released Saul's body."

"The funeral is set for Friday," she said. "Saul didn't want the usual. No sitting shiva for days afterward. Just bury him and move on, those were his wishes. The firm has promised to have a memorial service at some point."

Friday, the day after St. Patrick's Day. Not a good day for fathers.

"I'll be there," he said.

"Oh, that's not necessary…"

"It's the right thing to do," he said, "and…it's also good for the investigation."

She gave him a curious look. "Meaning?"

"Killers like to show up at their victim's funerals."

"That's morbid."

"Mostly they do it to assert their innocence. How could they mourn if they're responsible?"

"I don't understand people sometimes."

"Hell, I don't understand people any time."

She drank from her bottle. "I guess I didn't know Saul. I don't seem to know Harris either."

"Have you heard from him?"

"No," she said, her voice cracking. "I've called him several times, but it always goes to his voicemail. I think I called to hear his voice, even if he's asking to leave a message. Just like it's done for the past three weeks. Which is why we hired you to begin with."

"I saw him again. I told him to call you."

"Thank you, Jimmy. You're very kind."

"Now isn't a time for either of you to be by yourself."

Silence filled the apartment as the rain splattered against the window. Dreary weather had a way of making people feel alone.

"You know where he is. You could just go to the club," Jimmy said.

She shook her head. "I'm not controlling like Saul. When

Harris is ready to come home, I'll embrace him as though nothing has happened. But he has to want to come home. For now, I'm just happy to know he's fine, at least physically. And I have you to thank for that."

"Just doing my job," he said.

She set her empty beer down. Jimmy had barely touched his.

"I'll talk to Harris again. Perhaps I can bring him to the funeral."

She nodded. "I'll email you the details."

She rose from her seat, smoothing down her dress as Jimmy retrieved her coat and helped her on with it. She leaned over and planted a kiss on his cheek, a tender gesture from a woman who needed a connection, and offered just the right touch that Jimmy needed at this moment. He pulled away and stole a look back at the files spread out on the floor. Her eyes followed.

"Another case?"

"An old one, more of a mind puzzle."

"I hope you solve it."

Jimmy nodded. From her mouth.

"Thank you, Jimmy, for seeing me. I had to get out of the apartment, and I didn't know where else to go. I guess I just needed to see someone, anyone."

"Glad I could be anyone," he said with a sly grin.

After Jellison had gone, Jimmy realized he was drained. Physically and emotionally. It had been a day filled with questions and devoid of answers. He thought about cleaning up the files, but he left them just as they were, as though airing them out might wipe away some of the cobwebs and shed new light on whatever he was missing. He'd probably leave them that way until after the anniversary.

Putting on his coat, he turned the lock and headed out.

The noise coming from Paddy's was joyous, everyone preparing for St. Patrick's Day.

He kept walking, the rain dousing the fire in him. What he sought was comfort, and he could only find that one place. He kept a cautious eye out as he walked home, looking to see who might be lurking in the shadows, but all he saw was his own paranoia. He made it home safely and took the stairs two at a time, not even winded when he reached the top floor. When he pushed the door open, he found the apartment dark.

It was supposed to have been his mother's early shift at the theatre, but maybe a problem had developed and she'd stayed. He made his way into the apartment and was about to remove his coat when he noticed a small flicker of light coming from the kitchen. He walked in and found Maggie sitting in her usual seat at the table with a lone candle occupying the center. She was staring forward at the empty space opposite her. He noticed the glass that always stood there had been filled, the foam of the beer dissipating like lost memories.

Jimmy said nothing as he took his regular seat as quietly as he could. He felt pain reach deep into his tight throat. Maggie reached for his hand, finally connecting. Having a shared moment, a shared experience, together the two of them sat and remembered. They remembered a man who had been filled with life—zestful, honest, urgent, and capable. Honorable. A man who would have done anything for his family, had he been given the chance.

Life turns, its changes unexpected. Sometimes you took them as they came. Sometimes they took you.

How long they sat in silence, Jimmy couldn't say. The votive candle burned down and the beer grew warm, and the moment strengthened the bond between mother and son. But as Jimmy watched the dying flicker of the candle, he thought not of Joey McSwain, not of widowed Maggie and the fatherless teenager he had been. He saw Saul, Jellison, and Harris, another family broken apart by violence.

Sometimes life was nothing but a mystery. Solutions hidden in the dark.

The candle went out.

§ § §

"Thanks for meeting me."

"You make it sound so formal. We've shared ourselves. We've…"

Jimmy nodded. "Right."

He chastised himself inwardly for his poor opening salvo. He was nervous about meeting Barry, and while he usually prided himself on the nonchalance he brought to his paramours, an uncertainty swirled in his guts tonight. Maybe it was because Barry was the first guy he'd met in months who he actually wanted to do more than just screw. But if they were to move to a place beyond the physical, Jimmy had to come clean about his behavior that night. Sure, he could blame it on Harris's phone call, on the shocking news of Saul Rothschild's murder, but the truth of the matter was it had started before. Barry had pushed when Jimmy didn't want to be pushed. Barry had made what he thought was an innocent remark, and Jimmy had acted like a crook at his indictment.

They'd chosen a coffee shop rather than a bar. Keep their minds clear.

It was Wednesday night, just past eight, and the sky had darkened to a blue-black hue, yesterday's rain having moved on. As they took seats at a place called Joe on the Upper East Side, not far from where Barry had found a sublet on 75th and Lexington, mutual smiles crossed their faces. Jimmy was glad to be in his company, and Barry seemed to feel the same way.

"You want to tell me why your face is that shade of purple? It makes when we met look like nothing."

"Had a run in with someone. He won. For now."

"I see that," Barry said. "When did it happen?"

"Saturday night. Stupid me, I wasn't paying attention. Someone jumped me."

"Who did it?"

"That's the question of the week," Jimmy said.

He couldn't blame the cops for non-activity this time, it would have taken Jimmy filing a report to even have the cops make it an official case. He knew it would go the way of most cases like his: lost in red tape, not enough manpower around to investigate every assault. They would say they had more important cases to solve--robberies, rapes, murders.

"I wish you had told me."

"I didn't need false sympathy."

"I wouldn't have been false."

"No, but it would have been forced."

Barry offered up no answer that time.

"So, maybe I met you at a bad time," Barry finally said, a wistful look to his eyes.

"I'm not sure anytime is a good one to meet me," Jimmy offered.

They sipped quietly at their lattes, a dollop of whipped cream coating the stubble on Jimmy's upper lip. Barry reached over and swiped away the stray foam, licking it off his finger. Their eyes locked, and that's when he knew that Barry still orbited his world. The strong gravitational attraction between them remained, though their desire was only on simmer until Jimmy explained himself. He wasn't even sure where to begin. How do you explain the irrational?

You just jump in.

"In two days, it will be the fifteenth anniversary of my father's death," Jimmy said.

"Oh, wow, Jim…"

"Like I said, I don't need sympathy of any kind, not now. It's reality, for some history."

"But not for you."

"He died in my arms. I was fourteen."

"Oh…shit."

Yeah, that response worked, succinct. "He was a cop, killed by some stupid street thug."

"Why were you there?"

"Because my father was off duty. Wrong place, wrong time, so the cops say."

"His killer...what, is he about to be paroled? Is that what's got you...freaked?"

"I wish," Jimmy said. "His murderer was never found."

Barry slid his hand across the table, grabbing hold of Jimmy's fingers. The connection was tenuous, but it existed. Jimmy didn't pull back like he normally would have. He was talking, spilling his guts about having witnessed his father's blood pour out over Manhattan cement. It wasn't something he usually talked about with boyfriends. He'd told only one other man he'd been involved with. The only man he'd also said those three little words to.

"This time of year, I get kind of moody. I think about him a lot."

"Is that why you're a private eye? You want to find his killer?"

Jimmy wished they'd gone to a dive bar so he could hide himself in its dim lighting. He could use a beer about now, chasing it down with a Jameson shot. Instead, he sipped his latte. But tonight wasn't about beverages, it was about the conversation taking place over one. It didn't go unnoticed that Jimmy had chosen a place called Joe.

"You're good, Barry, astute."

"We don't have to talk about this anymore if you don't want to."

"I owed you an explanation. You were nothing but kind to me."

"I sense there's something else bothering you," Barry said. "Your current case?"

What wasn't bothering him? Saul Rothschild's murder, the coming anniversary of his father's death, what to do about Jellison and Harris, the sorrow he'd seen on his mother's worn face, the man who'd attacked him, the cops who expected him to go to a funeral on the anniversary of his father's death and report back to them. He had the weight of the world on his shoulders, and what he most wanted was to forget it all. But he didn't want to use Barry, not like he had that first night they'd met, when Jimmy sought sexual release with the first man who smiled his way. He had been surprised he wanted to know more about Barry, so he had asked him out on the second date, foolishly mixing it with his case. Like he could multitask the good and the bad.

"I got my heart broken," he suddenly said.

"Who hasn't?" Barry asked.

Two simple words, but their resonance made Jimmy realize just how selfish he was being. Didn't everyone have a relationship that had once defined them, only to leave them scarred when it was over? Everyone has a past. It's how we deal with them that allows us to move forward or not. Jimmy hadn't done so, unable to open his heart again. But across from him was a man who was accepting of his flaws, his faults, all the wounds. Jimmy reached out his hand, connecting with Barry, his nails digging into the flesh of Barry's fingers. He looked over at him and found understanding in Barry's eyes.

"Jimmy, you don't have to tell me everything in one night."

The coffee shop was closing soon, and they were among the final patrons. Late night it was best to limit your caffeine intake, so the two of them left the establishment, emerging onto Lexington and casually walking uptown. The 6 train was just a few blocks away, but so was Barry's new place. Jimmy wasn't certain which direction they were headed, and he wasn't about to ask.

"Walk me home?" Barry finally asked.

"Sure, okay. It's nice out."

Silver moonlight had emerged from the clouds, and sparkling stars dotted the sky like sequins. Manhattan was alight with an air of romance, and its glowing power seemed to fuel the couple forward. Turning east, they soon arrived in front of Barry's building, a classic brownstone on a quiet tree-lined street. Even the wind was silent. The only sound they could hear was their own breathing. The two of them stopped before the steps, each at a loss for words.

Finally Jimmy spoke. "I guess I'll see you, later."

"The next few days, they'll be all about family, right?" Barry asked.

Jimmy nodded. "St. Patrick's Day and the next, what I always called St. Joseph's Day."

"That's a nice honor," Barry said. "Will you call me…you know, after?"

"Yeah, I'd like that."

Barry leaned in, pressing his lips against Jimmy's. Jimmy felt the ache in his heart begin to heal. He wrapped his arms around Barry, drawing him in closer, their kiss growing more intense. A longing built up in his heart and in his loins, and when at last their bodies parted, their eyes didn't.

"Come upstairs," Barry said, his hand caressing Jimmy's cheek.

Jimmy gulped, the lump hard in his throat. This wasn't how he'd intended the night to go. Sometimes you had to let the apology sink in before you gave in to baser desires. Wasn't it too soon? But Barry's expression was earnest, his eyes flaring behind his glasses.

"You sure?"

"Why wait for tomorrow? There are no guarantees."

It might have been a phrase Jimmy would say.

Jimmy reached for Barry's hand, felt the connection, felt the growing heat.

They walked up the steps. Once inside Barry's studio apartment, they closed the door, and their bodies entwined, Jimmy pushed Barry up against the wall, their kisses intense. They left clothes in their wake, falling to the bed naked, heated, hungry.

Eyes locked again, Barry's urged his hairy lover to pleasure him. Again, his legs pointed toward the ceiling, Jimmy positioned atop him. He guided his cock toward Barry's ass.

When Jimmy entered him, Barry's eyes widened and he cried out, digging his fingers sharply into the muscled flesh of Jimmy's back, something he remembered Barry enjoyed doing. Except tonight it felt sort of stale, a trick already revealed. Still, this was pure bliss, the kind of pain he could live with. Jimmy fucked him hard, releasing his inner frustrations over the case. He thought about poor, tortured Harris, he thought about the caftan-clad Terence, and finally his mind drifted to Frisano. In his mind, Jimmy was unbuttoning Frisano's shirt. He imagined an endless dark carpet that he lost himself in.

"Oh shit...oh shit," Jimmy exclaimed, and seconds later he shot his load. He pumped at Barry until the last drop had seeped out of him, and as he pulled out and lay back, he realized he'd left his partner unsatisfied. Barry climbed atop him and began to stroke his own cock, his hard shaft red hot. It didn't take him long, and soon an eruption of come shot out over Jimmy's chest. He stared at it and again his mind went to Frisano and felt a wash of shame.

Afterwards, as they lay entwined in the tangled blankets of the bed, their bodies satiated, satisfied, coated with a silky sheen of sweat, Barry slept with his head against Jimmy's chest. Jimmy stared guiltily at the ceiling, knowing he'd fucked one man while dreaming of another. Why did everything have to be so fucking complicated? Why couldn't the uncertainties of future tomorrows be quieted in the dark secrets of the night.

Such peace was rare, Jimmy knew all too well. So of course it couldn't last.

He just didn't expect it to happen so quickly.

The sudden shattering of glass from the window facing the street jolted him out of the bed, its violent sound magnified by the silence.

Chapter Fifteen

"Who would do such a thing?"

"That's the question of the day, and the day's not even really begun."

St. Patrick's Day was a mere three hours old, and violence had already reared its ugly head. A lone light from the kitchen lit the room with shadows, allowing Barry and Jimmy to see the broken pane of glass. They walked carefully to avoid cutting their bare feet on the shards of glass that littered the hardwood floor. Barry pointed to the ordinary red brick that had caused the damage. Jimmy told him to keep back, even though the apartment was small without much space to maneuver.

"Wait here," Jimmy said, reaching for his clothes.

Small daggers of glass fell from the window and tinkled to the floor as Jimmy put on his jeans and his shirt.

"Where are you going?"

"Downstairs."

"You mean, like, outside?"

"I'm an investigator, I'm going to investigate."

"What if whoever did this is down there?"

"All the better."

"Jimmy, this isn't funny. I've…I've never been the victim of violence. I think we should call the police."

"It sucks, but you survive. The city hardens you. You fight back."

Tough guy words for sure, but inside Jimmy was apprehensive. He was not one to believe in coincidence, and so a second attack on him in the same week could mean only one thing. He'd pissed someone off. At least now he knew the beating he'd taken in the alley near his home hadn't been a random act. He'd been targeted. No more playing the innocent. This time he was angry.

Jimmy slipped on his shoes and kissed Barry before stepping out.

"Be careful," he said.

"Always."

"Said the man with the large bruise on his face."

"Don't turn on any more lights."

Jimmy tried a smile one could call rueful. Then he started down the stairs, taking them as quietly as possible so as not to wake any of Barry's neighbors. Perhaps one of them had heard the crash, maybe even witnessed something. It was doubtful at three in the morning, but then again, this was New York and people kept strange hours. Still, he approached the front door with caution, planting his body against the wall and peering through the glass of the front door at the street below. He waited patiently, he watched, and ultimately discerned no movement. Not only did no one appear, no car drove by save for a lone taxi, its dome lit. It sought passengers at a time when most slept.

At last he turned the knob and went out into the cool night. Bags of garbage were piled at the curb, cars lined the street, trees stood like sentries. If he was here, his assailant could easily be hiding behind any one of these objects. Had he remained behind to check the results of his handiwork? One thing Jimmy did know: the guy wasn't trying to kill him, just sending a message. But what was it? He thought of Saul Rothschild and the seemingly random blast of a gun that had claimed him. His death had been quick. He doubted Rothschild knew what had happened, and if whoever this guy was really wanted Jimmy dead, he was certainly enjoying taking his time.

He listened to the silence to see if it was going to give up any sound. Like the shuffle of feet, a cough, any scrape or sound another person would make. But nothing hit his ears, and Jimmy had to assume the guy had run off the moment he'd thrown the brick through the window. Walking down the steps, he stared up from the sidewalk at the third floor window. A thin shaft of light framed it, allowing him to see the jagged damage from the street. Part of Jimmy was impressed. The guy had amazing aim. Had he missed his target, it might have just hit the side of the building, or worse, a neighbor's window.

Suddenly Jimmy spun around, doing as Barry had asked, watching his back.

Had he heard something? Someone?

A young woman walked down the street on wobbly legs, and not from the heels she wore. She couldn't be any threat. He let her pass, but after she left, Jimmy noticed one of the brownstones across the street was under construction. On the sidewalk in front of it was a wooden pallet loaded with bricks. He ambled across the street, careful to look both ways and not because of the potential traffic on this one-way street. He wouldn't let the guy ambush him a third time.

As he came to the pile of bricks, Jimmy looked for any gaps where one might have been taken. While he couldn't be sure, coincidence seemed to be on his side.

The idea the brick had come from the pile said to Jimmy that impulse had driven his assailant. Maybe he and Barry kissing on the street had caught the attention of some stranger, a homophobe witnessing the heated PDA between two men. But even as he thought it, he didn't believe that was the motivation.

At last Jimmy returned upstairs, swept into Barry's arms the moment he closed the door.

"Oh, thank God. I was so scared. I think I still am."

"Whoever did this is long gone. No surprise really. A chicken-shit act for a chicken-shit coward. Letting his violence speak for him."

"Should we call the police?"

Jimmy shook his head. "They'll just take a report. They'll never find who did it."

"And you will?"

"I'm very good at my job, Barry," Jimmy said, "and I have the one thing the cops lack. Determination."

Jimmy reluctantly broke from Barry's clinging embrace, but not before kissing him. He grabbed for his cell phone inside his jacket pocket and flipped it open, taking pictures of the crime scene. The window, the glass on the floor, the brick. He asked Barry to get a Ziploc bag if he had one, and luckily he had them in several sizes. Jimmy used a towel to handle the brick, dropping it into the plastic bag to keep it from being compromised. Maybe Roscoe and Dean could do an analysis on it and see if they could pick up a print. Satisfied he'd collected enough evidence, he and Barry set about cleaning up the glass and boarding up the window with a cardboard box and tape.

"I'll call the landlord tomorrow to find out who does repairs."

"Send me the bill," Jimmy said.

"Jimmy…."

"This one's not on you, Barry. If it turns out it's a result of the Rothschild case, I'll bill the client."

At last the drama of the night had passed, and the two men slipped back into bed, each of them burrowing beneath the blankets trying to find comfort again. It was late, dawn rushing toward them with each turn of the clock. They tried to sleep. Barry held him tight, their bodies sharing heat. Even so, he shivered.

"Your world scares me," Barry finally said, his words floating between them.

"Yeah, sometimes it scares me, too."

Jimmy McSwain hated the honesty the darkness forced out of him.

§ § §

It was the same every year for Jimmy McSwain. As inevitable as the arrival of the vernal equinox was, the calendar first turned its attention to the celebratory St. Patrick's Day, the fourteenth such anniversary that would take place without the presence of Joseph McSwain, Jr. It was a day of mixed blessings for the

McSwains. Maggie spent the morning at church, Meaghan at her side while Mallory went to the law firm, the holiday just another long work day for her, leaving Jimmy conflicted on whether he would attend the annual parade.

Some years he went in tribute to all his father had stood for, saluting the blue line of cops who marched in solidarity. Other years, he buried his pain at a barstool inside Paddy's. To mark the tenth anniversary, a twenty-four year old, newly minted private investigator with untapped anger, Jimmy found himself at the parade but unable to salute. Bitterness at their inactivity on a case so cold it was as frozen as the day washed over him as he watched the cops who refused to let it thaw parade up Fifth Avenue with the false pride of being among New York's Finest. One thing remained constant however—each year he ended the day on a bar stool at Paddy's, burying the pain that would come with the new sun.

He'd left Barry's earlier that morning, telling him to try and have a good day. "Don't think about what happened. It might have been a simple prank."

"When will I see you again?"

He kissed him. "Trust me, I'll call you. Or you call me. No pressure, huh?"

"Stay safe. Trouble seems to enjoy your company more than I do."

Stay safe was the command that reverberated inside his mind as he contemplated the parade. Would he be safe among the throngs of people who lined Fifth Avenue, or would he feel more exposed, his assailant able to lose himself in the crowd after striking. He was determined to go either way, if not for the memory of his father, but to possibly flush out whoever had targeted him. The sooner, the better.

That's how he found himself on the corner of 48th Street and Fifth Avenue at just past eleven o'clock on that sun-drenched morning. Parade revelers were dressed in assorted hues of green. Some had painted their faces with shamrocks and wore T-shirts that said "Kiss Me, I'm Irish." Some carried tiny Irish flags and waved them wildly, their cheers already slurred from early indulgence.

Jimmy slid in between a few women who gave him cheerful smiles. He smiled back.

As the crowd around him jockeyed for position, forward momentum landed him against the metal barricade. He grabbed the bar and settled in to watch. Bagpipers marched on, their wail as soulful as ever, drowning the city in their cry. A succession of groups followed them: men in kilts, women tossing batons into the sky, revelers waving, cars honking. It was all a perfect sea of green, a celebration caught under the lush blue sky and gentle temperatures. Finally a row of uniformed police officers appeared in the shadow of St. Patrick's Cathedral, marching in step, flanked by the mayor and the police commissioner. In the front row just feet from the politicos, Jimmy noticed Francis Xavier Frisano, as clear a sign as any this guy was on the Fast-Track to One Police Plaza. He looked crisply handsome, sharp in his freshly-shined boots and dark blue uniform. He'd cut his curly dark hair for the occasion, it seemed, but his face still bore the shadow of his heavy beard.

Jimmy did like a man in uniform.

He thought Frank Frisano was one he'd like to see out of uniform.

It wasn't a complete betrayal of Barry, because he knew it was pure fantasy.

Jimmy McSwain would never get involved with a cop.

Frisano apparently had noticed him, giving him a slight nod of his handsome face. It was a subtle, sexy move.

And then the police officers had moved on, replaced by a float advertising trips to Ireland courtesy of Aer Lingus.

Jimmy considered it a commercial break, so he took that opportunity to leave. Walking back toward Hell's Kitchen, he realized he hadn't saluted the police, unsure if that was a subconscious decision or he was distracted by Frisano. He had kept his wits about him, and he'd seen nothing untoward, not a hint that he was being followed or singled out. His assailant's pattern was to strike at night, as though he sought anonymity in the dark. Or perhaps he had a conflict during the day.

As he made his way toward Paddy's Pub for what would certainly not be his last beer of the day, he thought of his father's footsteps. How the day before his father died, he'd marched proudly among his fellow officers, how afterword he would have journeyed back home to the west side, taking up residence on a barstool at his brother-in-law's pub to enjoy the remainder of the day's festivities with Ralpie and friends. Jimmy realized that's exactly what he was now doing, retracing his father's every move. One thing was different. His father had not carried a cell phone, and at that moment, Jimmy felt his vibrate. Harris Rothschild was calling him.

"This is Jimmy."

"Hi, uh, it's…"

"Harris, yes I know."

"Actually, it's Miss Jellicle Balls."

Ah, interesting turn of events. "What can I do for you, miss?"

"I'd like you to come back and see the show."

"Any particular day?"

"Tonight," he said.

"Special occasion?"

"Well, we are having a St. Patrick's theme. St. Patricia will be performing."

"I'm almost afraid to ask."

"Please say you'll come."

He thought there was more to it than just a simple invite. "What's the catch?"

Harris hesitated, as though searching for the words or perhaps just the bravery to speak them.

"Harris, tomorrow is your father's funeral. Is this somehow related to that?"

"Yes, I know," he said, "which is why you need to come tonight."

He knew what was being asked of him. "You want me to bring a guest?"

"Not the one you brought the first time."

"Let me guess. It should be a woman, and she should look remarkably like you."

"Like Miss Jellicle Balls."

"Oh, I thought that's who I was talking to."

This drag stuff sure got confusing. Jimmy heard a slight laugh from the other end.

"Thanks, Jimmy. Laughter is in short supply these days."

No argument there.

"I'll bring her, Harris, on one condition."

"What's that?"

"You call and invite her. She just wants to hear your voice."

"She'll hear it tonight."

Jimmy wasn't giving up, knowing Harris had to make some kind of overture. "Give her a preview."

Jimmy hung up without waiting for confirmation, satisfied that the Rothschild case had made some progress, though he wasn't sure he could take credit beyond trying to bond mother and son. Saul's killer remained at large, and neither Jimmy nor the cops had much of a lead beyond the gold Rolex they'd seen in the surveillance video. Still, with his help, Harris was planning to attend his father's funeral after all. That was the most important factor now, but it came with a condition—only if his mother first saw his act. God, he hoped Harris had the good sense not to come to the service in a dress.

Placing the phone back inside his pocket, Jimmy pushed past

a few smokers hanging out in front of Paddy's and made his way inside where the party had already started. His uncle saw him and waved him to the edge of the crowded bar, clearing the space for him. Paddy planted a kiss on each cheek, smiling warmly at him. Paddy knew what today was, rendering him all too aware of what tomorrow was. Family was a good thing to have, and a grateful Jimmy accepted a pint of Guinness. Together the two raised a silent toast to the man who should have been there with them.

Jimmy stayed longer than he had planned and drank more Guinness than he'd wanted. He had a chance to shake hands with Ronnie Gulliver, the man who had found him. He was tall and garrulous, with shiny dark hair. Jimmy bought him a beer, and the good neighbor slapped him on the back with hearty indulgence.

"Just looking out for our neighbors. You'd do the same," Ronnie said.

The joyous atmosphere at Paddy's had risen to new heights by three in the afternoon with the arrival of members of the local NYFD and a few of the boys from Midtown South. As much as Jimmy would have liked to stay, he had responsibilities. He needed to be sober for what the night's events would bring. But the best laid plans took a fresh turn as a surprising figure walked through the front door.

Jimmy was setting down his beer bottle when Captain Frank Frisano entered the bar. He was alone, and his eyes zeroed in on his prey. Frisano directed a curl of a smile at him that became broader as he made his way toward Jimmy. Jimmy felt his heart beat just a bit faster, knowing that the fast-rising captain had come seeking him out. He was still dressed in his parade blues, though he'd lost the tie somewhere.

"Captain, what brings you to Paddy's?"

"So formal, McSwain. I told you, you can call me Frank."

"Okay, Frank. So what brings you to Paddy's?"

"Same as what brings everyone, a beer."

"There's thousands of pubs in NYC. You walked into mine."

Frisano smiled over that one. "A few of the boys are on their way, guess I beat them," he said. "So, the owner's your uncle. Think you can cut through this crowd and buy me a beer?"

Jimmy waved over to Paddy, who finished serving a few drafts to a thirsty group before making his way over. Introductions were made, Frisano and Paddy shaking hands. "Welcome to the neighborhood. I know my stripes, you're a captain."

"Heading up the 10th."

"We're not on your beat."

"When I go north, I don't get nosebleeds," Frisano said.

Beers were poured, Jimmy realizing he had to order one, and soon he and Frisano had clinked glasses in a toast. With the bar so crowded and lively, the two men were practically pushed up against each other, so much so Jimmy could smell the man's expensive cologne. He looked away when he realized he'd been staring at a tuft of Frank's black chest hair sticking out of the top of his shirt. He looked like he had an impressive pelt, even more thick and plentiful than Jimmy's. Frisano hadn't moved , not his body, not his dark eyes.

"Any word on the Rothschild case?" Jimmy asked, uncertain of what to talk about.

"Roscoe's on it. I had to play bureaucrat today."

"You were in fine company at the parade."

"You want to play at One Police Plaza, you kiss whoever's ass you have to."

Jimmy wasn't sure how to take that remark. Was it just cop talk, or was their subtext to it?

"So, McSwain, this your usual hangout?"

"Like you said, my uncle owns it. Nice to have a relative in the booze business."

"Any other places you enjoy? More…intimate bars?"

He thought about Gaslight, and that of course made him think about Barry. Yet here he was in a straight Irish bar on St.

Patrick's Day with a very sexy, alluring Italian police captain who may or may not be hitting on him. Should he mention the gay bar and see what kind of reaction he got from Frisano? Or let him lead? Letting another man dictate the conversation was an unfamiliar role for Jimmy, but Frisano was not your ordinary pick-up. He hadn't gotten where he was by being careless.

"Neighborhood is full of interesting places," Jimmy said.

"Perhaps we'll have a drink at one of those interesting places...you know, some night."

"I'd be happy to show you around."

Frisano drank from his beer, finishing off nearly half of it in one gulp. As he smacked his lips, he said, "What makes you think I need an introduction? My precinct may lie in Chelsea but even Roscoe and Dean know the boys like to stretch their legs in other neighborhoods. Gaslight seems a nice place."

Did Frisano already know he hung there sometimes? "Musical Mondays," Jimmy said.

"Nah, I hate those sing-alongs. Couple of beers, a candle, some interesting talk. Who knows what else?"

Jimmy's mouth hung open for a moment as he tried to hide his growing desire for the man. He felt pressure in his jeans, even as words thickened on his tongue. He filled the silence by drinking his beer, saved from further talk with the arrival of a few loud, near-drunk cops who swept Frisano up into their group, wading deeper into the denizens of the bar. He just saluted Jimmy's way, their connection to be reestablished at another time, another bar. Left alone so abruptly, Jimmy wasn't sure what to make of that entire exchange. Had they agreed to go out on a date? If so, when? He thought he didn't date cops.

He let the issue go for now, setting down his beer. He'd had one too many and knew he had to keep his wits about him. Whoever had attacked him might want to finish the job. Eyes wary, he started back home to his mother's to take a quick nap and sleep off the affects of the murky stout before getting back to his case. It promised to be a long, eventful, perhaps emotional night. After that, St. Joseph's Day was going to stretch out forever. Time might be measured evenly, but the human mind could bend things, alter reality, giving the impression that the things you wanted to do slipped by quickly while those events you dreaded lingered long after you thought the clock should have turned.

Jimmy stopped suddenly. He was on the cracked sidewalk, standing beside a fire hydrant that stood curbside just beyond the entrance doors of the Happy Sons Deli. The hydrant had been there for years, protecting the neighborhood from fires and destruction longer than Jimmy had been alive, certainly longer than Joey had been dead. Yet what all these simple things had in common with was the fact Joey McSwain had been shot dead here, and Jimmy McSwain had held his father's body as his life slipped away. Jimmy might not have the chance to come here tomorrow, not with another funeral looming. Every year Jimmy made the pilgrimage, blessing himself at the exact time of the bullet's impact, here at the exact corner of the city.

"My vow remains, Dad. Maybe not today, maybe not tomorrow. Justice will prevail."

Jimmy always said belief drove him.

People walked by him, some glancing curiously. He paid them no bother. He might be on a crowded street in the beating heart of New York City, but for Jimmy, this was a private moment he shared with no one—not his mother or his sisters, and certainly not with strangers who had no idea of the loss he'd suffered.

The sudden vibration of his phone took him out of the shadows of the past and back to the present.

He stepped away from the fateful corner, answering his phone.

"This is Jimmy," he said.

"Thank you, Jimmy," came the trembling, vulnerable voice of Jellison Rothschild. "You gave me back my son."

He stared back at the sidewalk, seeing no sign of the blood that had stained it years ago.

The world had moved on, the unfair complexities of life winning out.

A world where mothers could get sons back. Sons. Not their fathers.

CHAPTER SIXTEEN

Sidewalks strangely offered up reflections of yourself, and of the world behind you. They held your shadow on sunny days, and on rainy nights, you could see a shimmering version of your inner soul. Jimmy had figuratively stared into one just hours before, and now it was Jellison Rothschild's turn to stare into hers. Before approaching the Dress Up Club, she asked Jimmy to take her to visit the exact spot her husband had met his destiny. He couldn't fault her, nor could he deny her. Didn't he still feel that way, even fifteen years later? Sidewalks were curious things, permanent pathways for transients. People always moved across them with no consideration for the lives that walked by or the imprints left in them.

Jimmy now knew of two square blocks of city cement where lives had been claimed, the bodies left to die as though their souls were trapped there until their killer was caught. Just as he felt his father's presence on that corner near his home, he imagined Jellison talking silently to her husband. It was wrong, all of it. Lives taken because of the violence of others.

At last, though, Jellison turned to Jimmy and said, "I don't understand why."

"The living seldom do," Jimmy answered. "Will you be okay?"

"I will, soon. When I look my son in his eyes."

Jimmy wasn't sure it was her son who would stare back.

She was quiet, staring at the sidewalk again. Then she nodded his way. "I'm ready. Let's move forward."

It was good advice and so, on a night when a streak of purple lined the sky and the hint of spring teased them, Jellison and Jimmy walked along Tenth Avenue until they approached the front entrance of the Dress Up Club. It was nearly ten o'clock, the night show soon to begin. When Jimmy peered in the window of the club, he saw a table near the front with a placard clearly marking it as reversed. The other tables were occupied.

"I think they're waiting on us," he said.

Jellison reached out her hand and touched his. "Thank you, Jimmy."

"It's Harris who wants you here."

"I'm nervous. I don't know if I'm prepared for tonight."

"Now you know how he feels. See, you both have so much in common."

More good advice, and she attempted to smile. It was the best she could manage. She looked great otherwise, a near sixty-year-old former starlet who had led a privileged life since meeting Saul Rothschild, spoiling her only child while turning a blind eye to the personal demons that sought to claim his identity. Beyond these doors he lived a different identity he'd found deep inside himself, inspired by the woman about to enter through them. Jimmy grabbed the handle, held it open and soon the two of them were whisked inside along with a sweep of air from the outside, almost like it had pushed them beyond the green curtain at the front.

Terry Cloth, still wrapped in her trademark robe, held her arms out wide as they walked in.

"Well, if it's not my favorite private dick," she announced.

"Not exactly the way to keep it private, is it, Terry, announcing my arrival?"

She planted a kiss on each of Jimmy's unshaven cheeks. "Ooh, I could just devour you."

Jimmy tossed a raised eyebrow her way. "This is Mrs. Rothschild," he said.

Terry curtsied like a proper lady. "An honor and a pleasure. If all of our girls' inspiration walked through the door…well, the place might just implode. But alas, no Cher tonight and no Aretha, and not the notorious Mrs. O'Leary…"

"I think she's dead," Jimmy said.

"Details. For St. Patrick's Day, one of the girls is trying something new."

"Let's hope she doesn't burn the place down."

"Honey, that was the cow's doing. You'll see," Terry said. "Come, your table awaits."

Their table was adorned with a white linen tablecloth and a single candle that flickered inside its sconce. A green carnation had been placed in a thin vase. Terry snapped her fingers and like the night Jimmy had been there with Barry, the shirtless waiter with a green bowtie approached with the same label champagne. He set it down, along with two glasses. Jimmy sensed all eyes falling on Jellison as the waiter bowed her way, wondering who she was and why the two of them were receiving the royal treatment. At last, the cork was popped, bubbly poured, and Terry moved on. She took the two steps to the stage.

The lights dimmed further, a spotlight hitting Terry just as she undid her robe to reveal a silky green dress that draped her shapely body all the way down to her matching heels. It could have come from the Emerald City, and for a moment Jimmy wondered if she were going to click her heels three times and send them all back home to Ireland. Terry just took a seat on a stool, crossing her fabulous legs. She smiled at the crowd, nodded slightly to the piano player, and serenaded the crowd with a lush, amazingly heartfelt version of the classic "Danny Boy." Jimmy sat mesmerized, listening and silently wishing his mother was at his side, especially on this holiday that celebrated her heritage. He could see already see the tears in Maggie's eyes because he had them in his.

It was a surprisingly beautiful moment and when Terry finished, the crowd collectively paused before the applause began.

"Thank you," Terry said. "A lovely way to start our special night."

Just then Jimmy felt his cell phone vibrating inside his jacket pocket. Patrons at a nearby table gave him a look of disdain at the buzzing sound. He let it go to voicemail, but a second later, it began to buzz again. Terry was talking to the crowed, and Jimmy stole the moment to pull the phone out, hiding it as best he could under the table. He saw the caller I.D.

Sissy Hickney.

Why was she calling? He was already on one case. Besides, wasn't hers completed?

He powered down the phone and put it away.

"Everything okay?" Jellison asked.

"It can wait," he said. "This can't."

Terry sang again, then she told a few off color jokes and by the time she finished her set, the crowd was in a festive mood. Urethra Franklin took the microphone and got everyone energized with a rendition of "It's Raining Men," and indeed out came the bartender and two waiters, each of them clad only in tight black pants, revealing bulging packages and chests waxed so smooth they looked oiled. Jimmy watched as the silly performance reached its crescendo, the guys tearing away their pants to reveal green thongs with a carnation placed in an appropriate spot.

The St. Patrick's Day theme continued for another half hour, with the aforementioned Mrs. O'Leary, who sang the old ditty about how her cow had sparked a blaze that nearly destroyed all of Chicago. It was ridiculous, even for camp, but the crowd ate it up. Of course, it might have been the free-flowing alcohol fueling the laughter. Jimmy drank his champagne, looking over at Jellison.

"I think it's called performance art," he deadpanned.

"I just want to see Harris."

"He's the closing act," he said. "One more to endure."

That was true, as Cher and Cher Alike came out, their act uninspired by the holiday. They did the same songs Jimmy had seen with Barry, but somehow it seemed excruciatingly longer. Jimmy's mind wandered, his eyes darting about the room. He hadn't forgotten that just a few days ago a man had been murdered near the club, that now his widow and his estranged son were moments away from meeting for the first time since the shooting. How would Jellison react when she got her first look at her son in character as Miss Jellicle Balls? And how about Harris? Despite the façade, the get-up, would his mother's presence rattle his nerves? So much had happened in the ten days since he'd closed the Hickney case and been hired by the Rothschilds.

His mind drifted to Sissy's phone call.

An odd feeling suddenly washed over him, and he had an urge to check his voicemail.

But he couldn't. Because Miss Jellicle Balls had just been announced. Jellison grabbed his hand, nails digging into the flesh of his palm. He caught her eyes, saw them filled with anticipation. Apprehension. He smiled at her, allowed her hand to keep the connection.

Then the curtain separated, the spotlight hit its target, and Miss Jellicle Balls emerged.

She was dressed in the same flowing red gown as when Jimmy had first seen her a week ago. And she'd been fabulous in what on Broadway they would call previews. Tonight was her opening night with her family sitting in the audience. She sat down, sharing the seat with her accompanist at the baby grand piano. He began to play, and Miss Jellicle Balls raised the microphone to her mouth.

Jellison 's fingers dug deeper. He absorbed the pain and hoped she didn't strike blood.

For some reason, such an image made him turn away from the performance on stage to face the front. He was thinking of the father who should be here and couldn't, his blood spilled so near. What he saw startled him. A man he knew all too well was pressed up against the window.

What the hell was Richard Hickney doing here?

Sweat formed on Jimmy's brow but he was stuck. No way to check his voicemail, no way to confront Hickney.

There was no way he could disrupt the performance. He

couldn't do that to Harris, or to Jellison. This moment transcended whatever Hickney's business was. Jimmy knew that even though the club was packed, the woman on stage was clearly performing for an audience of one.

Miss Jellicle Balls sang "Memory," and while the crowd sat rapt, tears slipped down Jellison's smiling face.

When it was over, applause filled the room and some members of the crowd stood, Jellison first among them. Jimmy did too. , not because he didn't find the performance worthy of an ovation but because he wanted to excuse himself. He whispered to Jellison, "I'll be right back," and made his way through the narrow space between the tables, negotiating his way to the bar. Seated at its edge, Terry Cloth tossed him an unhappy look, something he couldn't concern himself with right now. He didn't see Hickney. Had he just imagined him?

He found his way to the men's room and stared at himself in the mirror. It wasn't fear inside his eyes, more like uneasiness.

Reaching into his jacket pocket, he pulled out his phone. He had both a voicemail and a text. He opened the text first.

RICHARD IS COMING FOR YOU. BE CAREFUL. HE FOUND YOUR NAME IN MY EMAILS. HE BLAMES YOU FOR EVERYTHING.

Just then Jimmy heard a commotion back inside the club, followed by screams.

Then he heard the distinct sound of a gunshot.

§ § §

Jimmy had to act fast and think even faster.

Hickney might be after him, but if he was stupid enough to come after him in public, he might hurt anyone who got in his way. Hiding inside the bathroom was not an option, not only because it would leave him cornered and vulnerable, it wasn't his style. Not that he owned a gun, but his need to help the others had him thinking he would go out with his fists blazing. But that would only add fuel to the fire, he had to take a more stealth approach. Jimmy slipped out of the bathroom, the commotion from the crowd drowning out the squeak of the door. He peered around the wall and saw that the room was still filled. Richard Hickney , looking anxious, his eyes feral and possessed, blocked the front entrance. His gun was pointed up toward a neat hole in the drop-down ceiling. He'd only fired a warning shot. , perhaps he wasn't intending to use the gun, at least not on the club-goers.

"Nobody moves," he said. "I want you all to put your cell phones on the table. No one's calling the cops, no one's sending out any texts."

As Jimmy heard the clatter of phones upon the tables, he stepped toward the back of the club, seeing a thicker door with a small square pane at eye level. He knew it led to the interior of the building. He peered through the small window and saw the staircase that led up to the other apartments. Which meant just beyond it was the front door. Could Jimmy ambush Hickney from behind? Should he phone the cops?

He decided that second choice wasn't a choice at all.

No sense turning a disagreement with Hickney into a hostage situation for others.

Jimmy crept out of the club by the rear door, edging down the hallway and out into the noisy street. People walked by, their laughter fueled by St. Patrick's Day frivolity, all of them oblivious to the drama going on inside the club, or what Jimmy was planning to do. He needed to get past the large window in the front of the club without being seen by Hickney. He could crawl under the window, but the strange movement might call more attention to him. If he could get to the street, he could seek cover on the far side of the parked cars and approach from the south. Another group of revelers turned the corner and as they neared the club, making jokes about drag queens, pointing at the posters of the performers, Jimmy slipped into their group. He dashed behind a parked car, all without them taking notice. Heand doubled around it, keeping his body low. At last he was on the southern end of the Dress Up Club, next to a custom art and framing shop, all darkened.

He took a deep breath, knowing this was the moment of truth.

Finally he made his move.

He made a dash for the front door and saw the curtain billow open. Hickney still stood in the same place, blocking anyone from leaving. But he couldn't stop someone from entering, and that's just what Jimmy did. The rush of cool outside air caught Hickney's attention and he swung around, his eyes widening when he caught sight of Jimmy. He thrust the gun forward just as Jimmy leapt forward and crashed into him. Both men fell against one of the tables, a scream filling the room as they tumbled to the floor in a mess of broken glass. Jimmy clasped Hickney's wrist trying to get his hand on the gun, but a sharp object there kept him from getting a good hold, and Jimmy cried out with pain. He felt blood seep from the fresh wound. It wasn't a knife, just a bracelet of sorts, perhaps a watch.

A Rolex. A memory nearly blew his mind and he almost lost focus.

But that memory also helped him redouble his efforts. With one last burst of energy, he took Hickney's wrist and smashed it against the floor, dislodging the gun. He saw a hand reach for the revolver. A friendly one adorned with freshly painted nails. Hickney pushed back, and Jimmy remembered that he was strong. He'd gotten in that surprise first punch in during their scuffle in the alley behind Slings & Arrows. That wouldn't happen this time.

He raised his fist and brought it down on Hickney's face. A cry of pain filled the room.

"You bastard," Hickney panted, "you fucking ruined my life...I'm gonna kill you fucking Jimmy Mc..."

Jimmy didn't let him get to the Swain part. His fist connected with cartilage, and Hickney's nose crumpled into a squishy, bloody mess. Jimmy released his hold on Hickney, but not before banging his head hard on the floor. As he stood, wiping spittle from his mouth and trying to catch his breath, he saw Terry

Cloth with a pair of handcuffs.

"Don't ask," she said.

Hickney was soon cuffed to the handrail of the bar. Blood dribbled out of his mouth and nose, his face otherwise covered with a snotty sneer of disgust. Jimmy couldn't be sure if it was at his failure or just himself in general. Sirens wailed in the distance. Great. That's all he needed, the NYPD to the rescue.

As Jimmy looked out at the crowd, he said, "It's all right now, folks. Crisis averted."

The applause Jimmy received nearly rivaled that which Miss Jellicle Balls received.

Jellison came running up to him, hugging Jimmy and asking if he was okay.

"Yeah, I'm fine. Everyone else okay?"

"Looks that way."

Jimmy looked at Terry Cloth. "Sorry I had to disrupt the show earlier."

"If you hadn't, you would have been stuck inside just like the rest of us."

"Actually," he said, staring down at Hickney and resisting the urge to kick him, "I might be dead."

"Ooh, Jimmy, you're bleeding," Jellison said.

Jimmy looked at his hand and saw blood smeared against his shirt. "Just a scratch," he said dismissively. That's when he remembered the sharp object on Hickney's wrist, and when he bent down to examine it he found the biggest surprise of the night. He had the feeling he'd just solved two cases for the price of one.

Richard Hickney was wearing a gold Rolex.

As he stood up, he saw that not only was Jellison at his side, but so was Miss Jellicle Balls, aka Harris Rothschild, and she was enveloped in the comfort of her mother's arms. It was good that they were together, not only because their separation had been unnecessary, not only because their reunion here inside the Dress Up Club was ideal, but because he could present to them at the same time the killer who had fractured their family. At least they could have peace and justice. They could all rest.

"You two look happy," Jimmy said.

"Reunited," Jellison said, hugging her son tight. "You gave me my son back."

"Perhaps you've gained a daughter," Harris said, and then he addressed Jimmy. "Thanks. Others were paying you, but I felt you were always on my side."

His voice was strangely deep in light of the outfit he wore.

"I'm happy it worked out for the two of you. Jellison, if you ever needed proof of your son's devotion, look no further than his performance."

"He's far more talented than I am," she said, her smile widening, "and prettier."

Laugher enveloped them just as Terry Cloth joined the happy embrace.

Jimmy heard the sirens get closer. The police would want statements from everyone. Jimmy wished he could slip out into the cover of the night, avoiding the questions and the paperwork. The cops were not high on his list of priorities right now, but then again, they never were.

Midnight had come, and with its arrival, another St. Patrick's Day was over.

The fifteenth annual St. Joseph's Day was here, but the sun was not yet ready to shed light on it. For the moment, and only for now, Jimmy was just fine with his own darkness.

At the conclusion of every case, Jimmy liked to write up a file.

He was settled on the hard floor of his office above Paddy's Pub late on what he called St. Joseph's Day. It had been busy and highly emotional, and he could have just fallen asleep at his mother's after a dinner that left him overstuffed. He probably should have. Yet he had to set down the facts of what had happened at the Dress Up Club while they were fresh in his mind, and he set about his task with the determination that never left him. A cold Yuengling stood sentry next to him, condensation dripping, loosening the label. The window of the apartment was open wide, and as the hushed sounds of a hung-over New York settled in for an early night, warm temperatures hovered in the air. A sure sign that spring loomed.

Jimmy McSwain, relaxed and focused, was dressed only in a pair of baggy sweat pants. Stretching out his legs as he gathered up the various pieces of paper from which he'd jotted down notes throughout the Rothschild case, he fired up his computer. He stared at the empty screen. Soon it would be filled with pages of descriptions, thoughts, theory, and ultimately, facts. It was facts that closed a case.

The Rothschild case had been a seemingly simple one, complicated by murder and fueled by enmity.

But it had ended up being two cases bound by one common link: Jimmy himself.

He took a sip of his beer.

And then he began to type.

§ § §

Case File #609: HIDDEN IDENTITY.

It's all good now, but it almost wasn't.

With an assist from Mallory, I was hired to find the missing heir of her boss at the law firm that employed her. Saul Rothschild and his once-upon-a-time Broadway starlet wife Jellison, had not heard from their son, Harris, for over two weeks, and were worried he'd gotten caught up with the wrong crowd. Most people would assume that meant drug dealers or criminals, but in fact Harris had sought asylum at a drag club masquerading as a halfway house for those confused about their lives, their identities, and their sexuality. I'd found him, encouraged him to contact his parents, and given him twenty-four hours. Only one thing went wrong. Saul Rothschild didn't trust me and had me followed. Once he knew the location of his son, he took over. An argument ensured, Saul rushed out of the club at three o'clock in the morning and was promptly set upon by a man with murder on his mind.

Dressed in a dark hoodie but still wearing his street clothes underneath, including a gold Rolex he'd earned after ten years at his company, Richard Hickney shot Saul Rothschild dead by mistake, assuming he was me. He'd seen me enter the club at the start of the night, but had apparently missed me leaving in the arms of Barry. Lingering in the dark, nervous about enacting what his mind secretly desired, he saw a lone figure leaving the club, and that's when he jumped out of the shadows and fired without looking, without thinking. He'd dropped the gun out of fear and retreated back to the safe confines of New Jersey, where his wife, Sissy, was unaware of his nocturnal departure.

Apparently, Hickney had escaped his wife-imposed prison the night that I was attacked on the darkened streets of Hell's Kitchen. He followed through on what he'd missed out on doing that first night at Slings & Arrows. He confessed to the cops that he should have made sure I was dead that night, and he wished he still had the gun, as much as he enjoyed beating the crap out of me. He followed me another night, when I reunited with Barry and went to his home. Hickney threw the brick, as a warning, I supposed at first, but in the end what had motivated his string of crimes and his attempt at retribution was jealousy. Jealousy over being free to live life on my own terms, something Hickney couldn't allow himself. Whatever existed within him that disallowed him to be free inside his own skin, his anger became directed at those men who had no trouble loving other men, and of course he fixated on me and my relationship with Barry.

He had to wait a couple days to get his hands on another gun. Once he secured one, he set his deadly plan in motion. What better place to exact his final revenge than at a place where men dressed up as women to satisfy hidden identities within. I had been his target all along. Saul was a victim of circumstance, of his own distrust, the rash impulse of a man who never *gave thought to his actions.*

When the police arrived, I let them take over, Frank Frisano leading the case. Hickney was taken and later he confessed to everything, against the advice of his lawyer. But seeing the hurt in his wife's eyes, he knew he had to release her from his life and their marriage. In doing so, he was able to release himself from who he had been, who he had become. If only Hickney had sought help, if he had known about a house of refuge such as the one offered by Terence Black, he might have found peace. It still would have destroyed his family, his wife's life, and that of their young son, but it was one thing to be divorced, a weekend dad and gay, than to be an incarcerated murderer with no hope for parole. But that was for the Hickneys to figure out. I didn't envy him in the slightest.

Today I spent my morning graveside. Not the grave I expected to find myself at.

Standing in the background, while the spring sun beamed down and offered up fresh hope, Saul Rothschild was laid to rest as his devoted wife, Jellison, held a red rose that matched her lips, and at her side stood her son, Harris, his lips equally red. My sister Mallory was there, too, standing next to me. Just a few feet from us stood a couple of the senior partners from the law firm, their strong presence a phalanx of power. We all remained silent, respectful of the family's wishes. Saul was lowered into the ground, and roses followed suit, a sign of love, a sign of rebirth.

So the case was over, but no one was happy, no one was satisfied because of the hurt we had all seen.

The hurt I'd felt.

Nothing healed the wounds of yesterday more than the enveloping warmth and support of your family, and that's what I had. Ma cooked up a feast, and at the dinner table it was just family, the way it should be. Me, Ma, Mallory, Meaghan, and Uncle Paddy. The thought had occurred to me to invite Barry, but I had doused it, because things were cooling as he was getting settled in his job, making friends. Ultimately, it wouldn't have been appropriate, not on this anniversary. History said that the Irish and English didn't always see eye to eye to begin with, and if you add in the fact that the man with the funny accent that might have been at our dinner table was a lover of mine, it would have taken the luck of the Irish to survive one of Joey's rants.

I would have been just fine with that.

It would have meant Joey was with us.

For now, though, life moves forward. A new day dawns. New cases will always find me. New men will find me, too, or I will find them. Captain Francis X. Frisano comes to mind when my mind turns toward the personal. The rumored drink together had yet to come to fruition. Life had enough complications, the heat I'd felt between us, me the private eye, he the cop, remained chilled by an old case, a cold case.

One that will haunt me until I close it.

Tomorrow the Catholic Church celebrates the real Feast of St. Joseph's. The world could have that one. I had my own.

CASE 609: HIDDEN IDENTITY.

STATUS: CLOSED

ADAM CARPENTER is the author of many titles of gay romance, erotica, and mystery. His "Edenwood" trilogy includes EDEN'S PAST, EDEN'S PRESENT, and EDEN'S FUTURE. His "European Flings" trilogy includes the prequel short story, "Prelude to a Fling," followed by PASSION IN PARIS, RAPTURE IN ROME, and LUST IN LONDON. His "Wonderland" trilogy includes DESPERATE HUSBANDS, DESPERATE LOVERS, and DESPERATE ENEMIES, co-written with Curtis C. Comer and Jeff Wilcox. Other books include the "White Pine" series, SECRET FLAMES, HEAT OF THE MOMENT, A RAGING FIRE, and BURNING TRUTH, as well as the Johnny Lee Captone-featured DUDE RANCH and the novella-length A YEARLY TRYST. His short fiction has been collected in the anthology, NOCTURNAL DELIGHTS. Stand-alone novels include THAT PASSIONATE SEASON, SUMMER'S CHOICE, YOU OWN ME and ISLAND DESIRES. He is currently at work on the next Jimmy McSwain novel.

The author acknowledges the trademark status and trademark owners of the following wordmarks mentioned in this work of fiction:

Rite Aid – Rite Aid Corp.

Heineken – Heineken Browerijen

Jerry Springer – Multimedia Entertainment, Inc.

L'Oreal – L'Oreal Societe

Pabst Blue Ribbon – Pabst Brewing Company

Smithwick's – Diageo Ireland

Jameson's – Irish Distillers, Ltd.

Les Miserables – Cameron Mackintosh, Ltd.

Bass Ale – Bass LLC.

Penguin Books – Penguin Random House

Hugo Boss – Hugo Boss Trade Mark Management

Botox – Allergen, Inc.

Metropolitan Museum of Art – The Metropolitan Museum of Art Corp.

Guggenheim – The Solomon R. Guggenheim Foundation Not-for-Profit Corp.

Guinness – Diageo Ireland

Google – Google, Inc.

LinkedIn – LinkedIn Corp.

Twitter – Twitter, Inc.

Facebook – Facebook, Inc.

New York Mets – Sterling Doubleday Enterprises

Twinkies – Hostess Brands

Ding Dongs – Hostess Brands

Depeche Mode – Venusnote, Ltd.

Yuengling – D.G. Yuengling & Son

Coldplay – Coldplay Partnership, Ltd.

Atlanta Braves – Atlanta National League Baseball Club, Inc.

Coke – The Coca-Cola Corp.

Metrocard – Metropolitan Transit Authority Corp.

Budweiser – Anheuser-Busch, LLC

Florida Marlins- Florida Marlins L.P. DoublePlay Co.

Wizard of Oz – Turner Entertainment Co.

Rolex – Rolex Watch USA, Inc.

Ziploc – S.C. Johnson & Son

Aer Lingus – Aer Lingus LLC

CPSIA information can be obtained at www.ICGtesting.com
Printed in the USA
LVOW08s1148050614

388747LV00001B/9/P